ALFALFA FLATS

The two outlaws were on their way to Alfalfa Flats Staging Post to rendezvous with the rest of the Tindale gang when the rangers caught up with them. Ranger Mike Standler and his partner, Billy Barnes, pretended to be the outlaws and waited for the rest of the gang to show up. At the staging post they found an unsavoury piece of work called Carter and a ragged, half-starved kid whom Carter was supposed to be looking after. Billy Barnes made a friend of the boy, but that friendship was fated to cause heartache and bloodshed.

JACK GALLAGHER

ALFALFA FLATS

Complete and Unabridged

LINFORD
Leicester

First published in Great Britain in 2004 by
Robert Hale Limited
London

First Linford Edition
published 2005
by arrangement with
Robert Hale Limited
London

British Library CIP Data

Gallagher, Jack
    Alfalfa flats.—Large print ed.—
    Linford western library
    1. Western Stories
    2. Large type books
    I. Title
    823.9′14 [F]

    ISBN 1–84395–764–7

Published by
F. A. Thorpe (Publishing)
Anstey, Leicestershire

Set by Words & Graphics Ltd.
Anstey, Leicestershire
Printed and bound in Great Britain by
T. J. International Ltd., Padstow, Cornwall

1

Sandler wondered what was wrong. Then it struck him: it was quiet. Just the sound of hoofs shuffling through the dust, and nothing else but acres of silent desert. He looked round and saw Billy Barnes propping his Colt Peacemaker in the crook of his arm and thumbing back the hammer.

'You shoot that thing, Billy, it'll be the last thing you do this side of salvation, because I'm gonna put a bullet through your brain and save Caffrey and Stone the trouble.'

'Goddam, Mike, that old coney just about walked up to the side of the road and said, 'Hi, boys, I'm dinner'. That there jackrabbit couldn't be more obligin' if he took a knife and skinned hisself. Look at him sitting there twitchin' his ears.' Sandler glanced at the rabbit perched ready to run on a flat rock by the side of the track and said, 'Caffrey and Stone are half a day ahead, no more, according to the tracks. Let off a shot and next thing we know we'll be riding into their crossfire.'

'It's hardtack for breakfast, hardtack for dinner, and hardtack for supper too. Hell, I'm plumb burned out on hardtack, and I'm going to eat that crittur roasted if it's the last thing I do.'

'Not unless it dies of natural causes in the next five minutes, you ain't.'

'Well, let's just see about that.'

Barnes unhooked his lariat and shook out a noose.

''Fore I joined the Rangers, I used to work for a livin'. Roped and branded for some of the best outfits in the Panhandle. 'Member my partner Tommy-Joe McCauley fell off a butte up on the Lenora Plateau and, happenin' to have my waleline in my hand, I just sent a loop down after him, cinched him round the ankle bone, and hauled him the hell back up barely seconds before he splatted hisself on the rocks below. 'I reckon you done saved my life, Billy', Tommy-Joe told me, ''Cause round about the time you noosed me I'd about given up trying to think up a way out of that there fix'.'

Barnes whirled out a loop above his head then lobbed it with an easy swing of the arm. It was as if the rabbit and Billy had rehearsed this trick till they had it perfect: the rabbit turned and hopped right into the floating circle of manila rope, whereupon Billy gave a quick jerk, at which the rabbit made a graceful backward flip, then came sliding back home in a series of jerks as Billy neatly recoiled the lasso on his pommel. It seemed to dangle trusting and patient from Billy's left fist while Billy un-noosed it, flipped his Colt and caught hold of the barrel, then whacked it on the nape of the neck with the butt.

For the next two miles, Sandler listened to tales of Billy's ropemanship. By the third mile Billy's voice had just become a drone in the background of his thoughts until he realized that Billy was asking him a question.

'What?'

'I said if my eyes was deceiving me or is that smoke up to the north-west.'

Sandler squinted in the direction Billy pointed and saw a smudge against the sky's faded blue.

'Looks like campfire smoke all right.'

'You reckon it's them?'

'Best we act like it was.'

'I reckon you're right there, Mike. I'd sure hate to let them two boys get the drop on us. The reports give some of that gang out as mighty tetchy characters. What about that sheriff's deputy up on the Staked Plains? That weren't even funny what they did to him. Sticking his feet in the fire like that. Makes my toes kind of curl up just to think about it. I rode hossback long as I can remember. Why, put 'em all together, I don't think I've walked five miles all told since I was eleven. Stands to reason the soles of your feet get mighty tender.'

'OK, that might be a campfire up there, and our two boys might be sitting round it brewing coffee.'

'Why don't we sneak up and blast them?'

'We might blast a couple of innocent strangers, because we don't know what Caffrey and Stone look like.'

'We could ask them their names, then blast them.'

'And what if they say their names are Smith and McGonigal?'

'Well, I can think of one or two strategies we could use, but seein' as you're the cap'n and get two dollars more than me, I reckon it's up to you to fix us up a two-dollar plan to get us the drop on them there peckerwoods.'

'All right, here it is. One of us'll sneak up there among the mesquite till we've got them in the sights of a Winchester. The other will ride in and greet the camp. If it's them killers, I calculate that any stranger who rides into their camp won't ride out again.'

'Greetin' the camp sounds like my

work. I'm more naturally sociable than you.'

'OK. Wait here, best give me a full hour to find myself a good position. If they break camp before that, too bad.'

Mike kept his head low and wound through the mesquite towards the campfire smoke. Twenty-five minutes later he glimpsed the men squatting on either side of a fire drinking coffee. He edged closer until he was sure that if he had to shoot he wouldn't miss, then he settled down to wait.

One of the men spoke in a low voice, the other grunted and nodded but never made any reply or spoke himself. The silent one was big and rangy, very wide in the shoulders. When he got up and went to tend to his horse, he showed a yard of daylight between his knees as he walked. The only other person Mike had seen as bow-legged was his partner Billy Barnes. In fact, when the man grinned, Mike guessed that he and Billy had both done some riding herd, because neither of them had a front tooth in their head — a badge of pride to a cowboy, showing as it does that he's done his share of wrestling that armful of whirling hoofs that a calf turns into when it smells the branding iron.

The other man was a little shorter and more compact, and Mike could tell by the cast of his features along with the fair hair and blue eyes that he came from the same German stock as himself.

The sound of whistling drifted out of the mesquite and the two men looked up. They sat cradling their coffee cups as the tuneless whistling drew closer.

According to Billy Barnes, he'd only ever been fired off two jobs: once was for laying a smoking Bar-Z brand to the seat of a foreman who had a trick of grinning at him while making remarks that Billy never could quite hear: the other time, he claimed they let him go because he was tone-deaf and his singing made the herd morose.

'Hullo, the camp.'

The blond one lowered his tin cup and said, 'Hullo, yourself.'

Billy climbed down off his horse and tied it to the clump of mesquite where the men's animals were cinched.

'Mind if I hunker down a spell?' Billy squatted by the fire and wiped the dust from his face with his bandanna. 'Been on the trail three days. Headin' to Abilene. Hear tell they're hiring on the Lazy W. Pay good money on the Lazy W. Top dollar. Where you boys headed?'

'Up the trail a ways,' the blond said.

'You lookin' for work?'

The blond said, 'Nope.'

'Could get you a job over at the Lazy W. The owner, Isaac Salmon, cousin of mine married his sister. Figure he owes the family a favour for taking that goddam female off his hands. That woman has a tongue could gut a buffalo — make a Cheyenne brave lick dirt and whimper if she once got started on him. You boys cowhands?'

'We worked the cows a little,' the blond told him.

'Could tell you was cowhands just to look at you. Your friend's kind of quiet. I like that in a man. Can't stand these blowhards, sounding off all the time. My names Billy Barnes, what's yours?' Billy stuck his hand under the silent stranger's nose.

'My friend's a mute.'

'A mute? He can't talk?'

'That's right. His name's Bob . . . Bob Johnson. I'm Joe.'

'Joe?'

'Joe Smithson.'

'Bob Johnson and Joe Smithson, huh? What happened to Bob, he lose his tongue?'

'No, he got his tongue, but it don't work worth a damn.'

'Well, it's a right shame. Old Bob wouldn't have been no good on that job down out of El Paso. Got fired off of that job, because the foreman was a goddam music-lover. Only got fired off but two jobs in my life — once was for branding this goddam son-of-a-bitch of a foreman. He had a way of kind of squintin' at me and grinnin' . . . '

Billy yarned, and Joe and Bob sat cradling their coffee cups and staring into the fire, while hidden in the mesquite Mike stifled a yawn and quietly tried to take the kink out of his aching backbone. While Billy was filling his cup for the third time, Bob got to his feet and rolled with his bowlegged gait over to the horses — when he turned back, he had a revolver in his hand.

Mike laid the breach of the Winchester against his cheek. As he took aim, it crossed his mind that putting a bullet in the brains of Billy Barnes when his mouth had settled into its stride didn't necessarily prove a man a hardened criminal. Billy gabbed on while Bob crept up behind, easing back on the hammer as he came.

Mike drew a bead and fired.

2

While Bob went reeling, clutching his shoulder, Billy flung his tin mug at Joe and jerked his gun as he jumped to his feet.

'Drop it, you son of a fan-tailed muskrat.'

Joe eased away from the butt of his pistol and grinned. 'A fan-tailed musk-rat?'

'You expect me to draw fast and crack wise at the same time? You know what I'm getting at.'

Still grinning, Joe let his gun belt drop.

Mike came out of the mesquite with his Winchester levelled. He picked the two pistols off the ground and shook out the bullets, then went over to the mesquite clump where the horses were tied and had a look in the two sets of saddle-bags that had been dumped by their feet. There was nothing in them but some beans, some jerky, and the few odds and ends to be found in any travelling pack. He strolled back over and faced the two men.

'You ain't got a friendly way with strangers.'

'Seems to me you're the one's who're being unfriendly — shooting my partner like that.'

'It was either that or watch my partner lose a fistful of brains.'

'Old Bob there — you thought he was going to murder your partner? Hell, no. Old Bob wouldn't hurt a fly. He's just a big kid with a heart of gold. Truth is, old Bob's a little shy of some of that old grey mush and he don't think too good. How it is, we was working on a ranch down south of here a ways, and last week we upped and quit, and when we drew our pay Bob went straight out and bought that gun right off. He's so proud of that old Navy Colt. It's the first proper gun Bob's ever had. Why, Bob was only fixin' to show it to your partner, that's all. He's just like a young 'un with a new toy.'

'Gol' durn it, Mike, ain't you a'feelin' shamed of your no-good self? You all but blowed an arm clean off of Bob — and here's me too that ain't even introduced y'all like Christian folk. This is Bob Johnson and Joe Smithson.'

'Bob Johnson and Joe Smithson?'

'Kind of funny us having names like that.'

'What do you call yourselves when you're using your right names?'

'Them is our right names. I guess if we was gonna pick phoney names we'd've come up with ones that didn't sound so goddam stupid.'

'How does Caffrey and Stone sound?'

'Never heard of them two fellers.'

Billy Barnes spat in disgust.

'Goddam, it's gonna be a long day.'

'Yeah,' Mike said. 'We might as well make ourselves comfortable.'

He motioned Bob to come over to the fire and sit beside Joe. Mike squatted down facing them.

'Now, how about if we shuck the bull and you give me your names?'

'Well, my name's Joseph, and my partner here . . . he's called Roberto.'

'Aw, hell.' Billy flung his Stetson to the ground and stalked over to his horse.

'OK,' Mike sighed. 'Let me tell you how it is. We're a couple of Texas Rangers. They give us an assignment to track down Dan Tindale who busted out of jail in El Paso. We almost caught up with him in the town of Stanhope. Got there just after him and a couple of boys robbed the Union Bank. The gang took off in all directions so we couldn't follow all of them — you were the lucky ones. We know your names because the town barber heard the leader of the gang call you by them when he told you to head north. I don't figure your boss is so smart.'

'Dumbest thing he ever done was ride into Texas and start holdin' up banks. Goddam Yankee son-of-a-bitch.

Why, ain't he ever heard of Texas Rangers? Goddam, dad-blasted, low-livin' — '

The sound of Billy hissing and spitting like a green log on the fire rose from behind the mesquite clump. From the corner of his eye Mike caught a glimpse of something he took to be the jackrabbit flying through the air and heard a thump as it hit the ground.

'Now, you two boys is probably smarter than you look — '

'Hey, Mike — '

Keeping his Winchester on Joe and Bob, Mike glanced over their heads to where Billy's face, showing a row of empty gums, loomed over the mesquite.

'What's up?'

'You got a stone?'

'What?'

Billy held up his jackknife. 'This thing is blunt as hell. You got a sharpenin' stone?'

'I don't believe I have.'

'Where's that stone of mine? Goddam, I don't need to be madder than I am now.' Billy fell to muttering and rummaging through his saddlebags.

'Now,' Mike said, 'if you boys are smarter than your boss, you'll start cooperating.'

'There's the goddam thing. I knowed it was in there someplace.' Billy came out of his saddlebag with a hunk of whetstone in his hand.

'The way we are in Texas,' Mike said, 'we appreciate cooperative folk. Folk that give us a hard time, on the other hand, just make us madder than hell. So, where were you two boys heading? You got a place to meet up with the rest of your friends somewhere up ahead?'

'Like I said, we was just headin' up the trail a spell, no place in particular.'

'Mike, let me have that there Bowie of yours.'

Bob hadn't seemed to be paying much attention to anything but the hurt in his shoulder, but when Mike's knife slid from the sheath his eyes widened at the sight of the cruel twelve-inch blade. Mike gave the knife an easy flip over the heads of the two men and Billy grabbed the handle as it turned in the air.

'That pocket-knife is no damn good for skinnin'.'

'The teller that got shot died,' Mike said. 'You going to tell me who shot him?'

'This could do with an edge puttin' on it as well,' Billy said as he ran his thumb along the Bowie's blade.

Bob kicked Joe's boot and whined like a fretful hound.

'Take it easy, Bob,' Joe told him. 'Like I said, you boys got the wrong fellers.'

Over behind the mesquite, Billy began grinding.

Already badly rattled by his wound, Bob's face twitched at every stroke of the knife on the stone, while his eyes swivelled back in the sockets and showed their glittering whites. Whimpering, he flung another kick at Joe's ankle.

'I said take it easy, Goddam it,' Joe snapped — though he seemed to have caught a little of his partner's unease himself.

'Takes a good sharp edge for skinnin'.' Billy ground at the blade.

'What the hell's goin' on here?' Joe demanded.

'You think about answering questions, not asking.'

'I heard some of you fellers stuck a deputy's feet in a fire one time,' Billy said, grinding the while. 'I call that behaviour downright un-neighbourly.'

'What's he fixin' to do?' The tremor in Joe's voice drew another whimper from Bob.

'You keep talking but you don't say what I want to hear,' Mike said.

Billy laid the Bowie's blade against his cheek. 'Nearly there.' He spat on the stone and ground some more.

Joe and Bob were white-faced. Joe's jaw muscles twitched and Bob's eyelids flickered at each grind of the knife.

At last Joe shouted:

'All right.'

He drew a shaky hand over his face.

'Goddam . . . I heard about you Texas Rangers. All right . . . let him quit scrapin' that damn knife for a minute . . . my name's Tom Stone and this here is Abe Caffrey. We're with the Tindale gang.'

'Who's got the gold you took from that bank?'

'Sam Tindale's got it.'

'Where is he now?'

'I don't know. That's the low-down.'

'You just helped him to rob that bank, and said, 'That's OK, don't worry about our share, we're just happy to oblige'? Whereabouts you going to meet up and split the gold?'

'Carter's. We're going to meet at Carter's. It's a stage stop twenty miles north of here — in a place called Alfalfa Flats. Sam told us to meet him there.'

'When?'

'I don't know. Could be two days time, could be a week. We just figured to make our way there and wait up.'

'So the six of you all gonna gather at this Carter's?'

'That's right.'

'Goddam,' Billy yelled.

Tom and Abe jumped and cast nervous glances at the mesquite clump.

'I'm telling the truth.'

'Why the hell am *I* doin' this?' Billy yelled.

Billy came striding over and flung a bloody bundle at the feet of Stone and Caffrey.

'I reckon you two bird-dogs can skin this rabbit if y'all want a share of it.'

3

They headed back towards Rangers' Headquarters in Pinewood next day with their prisoners and in the evening they came to a farmstead where they were greeted by a friendly giant of a Swede. Carl Johansson lived alone; three crosses on a ridge marked the resting place of his wife and sons who'd perished in a Cheyenne raid twenty years before. Carl made them supper, then showed them the root cellar where Stone and Caffrey could be shut away for the night.

While Billy jawed with Carl, Mike took Stone and Caffrey down to the cellar. Stone turned talkative, but not out of friendliness: he'd taken a personal dislike to Mike, and it eased some sort of itch to brag to him about his evil deeds. He knew with the teller dead he would hang in Texas no matter what he said now, and he even told — his bulbous blue eyes fixed on Mike, hungry for a reaction — how it was him and Caffrey who had tortured the sheriff's deputy up on the Staked Plains. Mike didn't show any reaction. When evil was powerless, he didn't hate it — he'd seen plenty who hated it most then: screaming outside of jailhouses, from the backs of courtrooms, choking on their rage, set to beat and mutilate and kill.

When Stone finished talking Mike barred them in and went to sit with Carl and Billy on the porch. Soon Carl turned in; he was a farmer, used to rising before dawn, and it was past his bedtime. Mike and Billy sat and smoked and drank some of Carl's moonshine.

'You're worrying, Mike,' Billy said.

'I ain't worrying, I'm thinking.'

'Oh, it just looked to me like you was worrying. Me . . . never could worry, myself. I just ain't got the patience, I guess. And the only thing that ever gets me to thinking is females. Sometimes, for instance, I think about that Mary Curran that lives with her widowed ma in Galveston. Or did, anyhow. Heard she got married two months ago. Came awful close a couple of times to marrying her myself . . . awful close. I guess it's for the best — the thought of bein' under her orders put me off a mite. She married a retired army sergeant. She was kind of plain, but now that she's gone I can't help rememberin' what a good figure she had. Ah, hell, somehow I never could grasp that ol' matrimonial nettle — just can't take orders from a female, I guess . . . I don't believe I can take orders from anybody I can beat in a fight.'

'You take orders from me. How do you know you can't beat me?'

Mike thought that if Billy ever landed one of those big fists on him, it would be the last thing he'd know this side of creation.

'I might beat you if you was in the wrong, but I guess you're one of those fellers wouldn't start a fight unless they was in the right.' Billy scratched his head. 'I reckon worryin' keeps a guy steady. All the worriers I ever knew were steady guys. You're a steady kind of a guy, Mike. Me, I'm no steadier than a drunk injun trying to stand a floatin' log.'

Mike guessed it was true that he worried, but he wasn't sure he was as steady as Billy gave him credit for. He was like a river that flowed along nice and easy, day after day, so you didn't pay it no mind, until one day you woke up to find it had washed your crops away. Back in 1860, when war began to look as certain as ma's rheumatism after rain, he'd worried himself to a frazzle, then when all his friends had begun putting on grey coats, he'd woken up one morning, saddled his roan, and rode hell-for-leather north to join the Army of the Union. His pa had thought he'd gone crazy, but when the North won, pa thought he'd had it all worked out and was just playing it steady and clever all the time; because pa's lumber mill was about the only business round about that survived the Reconstruction. Then pa had to change his mind again when Mike told him he didn't want to take over the business, but was set to join the Texas Rangers instead. Pa thought he'd make him see sense by threatening to cut him off without a penny, but when he found that Mike was as locked on his craziness as a hound dog locked on a timberwolf's scent he turned thick-headed and made good on his threat, so Mike's cousin Henry had ended up getting rich selling pine sleepers to the Union Pacific while Mike drew twenty dollars a month and livery allowance.

'I wish you hadn't told me it was them two sons-a-bitches burned that deputy. Got me to tinglin' from the soles of my feet right up to the hollow side of my knee bones. I just can't figure out what puts a notion like that in a man's head, unless he's born Injun and then it's a kind of custom or tradition or such. But I ain't surprised it was Caffrey that first had the notion to do it. I can tell a guy's nature just by lookin' at him — gener'ly, the uglier they is the worse they is, and that mute is one ugly-lookin' son-of-a-bitch. He puts me in mind of a feller I met back in sixty-four. I 'member . . . '

Stone had grinned as he told about the deputy, but Caffrey had shown no reaction, just sat there hunched and surly with his dull eyes staring at his boots. He hadn't got much in the way of brains by the look of it, and what thoughts passed through them seemed of a resentful cast. No doubt the chip on his shoulder was to do with being mute. Probably to him, a tongue was first and foremost a weapon, and he felt the lack of his mostly as a chink in his defences. Even with a tongue he wasn't a type to inspire liking, or interest, or sympathy: the only way he could win any notice at all was through fear; no doubt like most of his breed he thought kindness was another word for foolishness, and looked to depend on ruthlessness alone to win any kind of respect.

Stone just flowed like water. What stood in his way he'd go round. Blocked, he would back off, feel for an easier channel. If the ground was in his favour he'd come on strong and fast, pound you to pieces. Otherwise, he didn't push too hard — just waited, like deep water waiting for your canoe to spring a leak far from shore, ready to swallow you up. As Stone talked to him, looking at him sideways out of his bulbous eyes, he'd got the creepy feeling of Stone's mind or spirit or whatever-the-hell flowing around him, searching out the crannies of his character. He imagined him now, hatching up some plot, some trick to throw on the road. It was a long way back to Pinewood ... Imagination — his people weren't supposed to have too much of that. He had plenty. And Stone had too. Stone was the same age as him, the same build, had the same

Bavarian looks. They were like matching pieces of a jigsaw: alike in some ways, completely opposite in others. And there you had Caffrey too: he was just like Billy in some ways — though different as hell in one.

' . . . Goddam, Mike.'

'What?'

'I'm 'bout startin' in to get some sympathetic feelin' for that feller Stone — teamed up with a mute like he is. I asked you the same question three times now, and I'm no closer an answer.'

'What is it?'

'Well, it don't even seem worth it now. It's just when a feller puts a question, it kind of frets him not to get an answer, and I was just askin', so's you wouldn't feel out of the conversation, if you wasn't worryin' but thinkin', then what the hell all was you thinkin' about. But I kind of lost interest myself now, so forget it.'

'Well, Billy, I'm glad you asked me that question, just so happens. I was thinking what if, instead of taking these two outlaws back to headquarters, we were to leave them here and take a ride out to Carter's stage post?'

'You mean bring Carter in as well as an accessory?'

'No, I mean wait there till Tindale shows up.'

'You said Stone told you Carter had a signal he would use to show the gang that it was safe to approach the house. We gonna have a problem there unless we can get it out of Stone what the signal is. Hey, why don't I go down and threaten to put a bullet in him if he don't tell?'

'Stone's going to hang anyway. He knows that. If he did talk, he could as easy lie.'

'Then we threaten this Carter we'll open him up if he don't tell?'

'He could as easy lie too. If Tindale didn't show up, how would we know it was because of a signal or because the rangers chased him into Mexico?'

'So, what's the good of going the hell

out to Carter's place?'

'We go and tell Carter that we're Stone and Caffrey.'

'Hmm . . . ' Billy sucked his gums. 'You think we could make him swallow it?'

'According to Stone, Carter's never seen them. What say you grab that lantern and I'll take this corn jug and let's go chew some more fat with Stone?'

Stone put a hand over his eyes to shield them from the light and told them they could get lost because he wasn't in the mood to talk any more.

'We just come for a friendly chat,' Mike said. 'Brought you a jug of moonshine.'

Stone squinted at the jug, then said, 'What the hell, let's chat.'

'Kind of like to know about any other jobs you done so we can clear them up,' Mike said. 'Tell us, and I'll leave the jug.'

'Well, OK . . . gimme a drink on account.' Stone told them about two banks and a gambling hall they'd robbed in New Mexico and how they'd cleaned out an army suttler's store and raided a horse ranch in Texas.

Then Billy said, ''Bout this here Carter — what's this here signal he uses to let you know it's safe to approach?'

'He don't use no signal when it's safe to approach, he uses a signal when it ain't safe. And I ain't telling you what it is. You can keep your corn. Tindale let us nominate somebody for our split if we was caught or killed. I gave my mama's name. She ain't a bad old girl, it weren't her fault I went wrong, so she might as well have mine. Besides, if Tindale's free, he'll try to bust us out before they get round to hanging us. He swore his word on that, anyway. At the moment I'd rather believe him than not.'

'You should have had a signal to say it was safe to come in,' Mike said. 'Otherwise, how the hell was Carter going to know who you were? I knew your boss couldn't plan worth a damn.'

'What difference does it make if he

knows us or not?'

'You just going to turn up and say, 'Hi, I'm Stone and this is my partner Caffrey, we're in Tindale's gang'?'

'Why not? He knows our names. What else does he need to know? He knows Abe's a mute. Before the job, Tindale sent a Mexican kid to warn Carter to expect the six of us. He was to tell Carter we could arrive any time over the next two months, all together or piecemeal. The kid would tell Carter our names and what we looked like. What else does he need?'

'Yeah, I guess you're right. OK, well, enjoy your corn. You can have a good long lie tomorrow.'

'It just might work,' Billy said after they'd barred up the root cellar. 'Yeah, we ride up there and I tell Carter I'm Tom Stone and this here's my partner Caffrey.'

'I thought I'd be Stone.'

'Hell, no. You're natural to play the part of a mute — laconical son-of-a-bitch like you.

'You don't look like Stone.'

'Well, I sure don't look like Caffrey.'

'We gotta chance it. Stone's fair like me, and you and Caffrey are dark.'

'How in hell could I ever pass for that plug-ugly mute?'

'Just keep your jaw shut and . . . I don't know . . . try to look ugly.'

'Try to look ugly. Goddam, that's about the dumbest thing I ever heard.'

4

Carl Johansson was ready to oblige by keeping Stone and Caffrey in his root cellar.

'Don't take any chances with them bird-dogs,' Mike told him. 'Leave some grub by the cellar hatch once a day, draw the bar and call them up to collect it, and meanwhile you stand at a safe distance ready to blast them if they make a suspicious move.'

'Can count on me, boys,' Carl said. ''Dese two fellers don't worry me, no sir. I open them wide open if they try a ting.'

They rode for two days, and as the sun was setting on the third they came upon a sign that said: Alfalfa Flats Staging Post. 5 Miles Ahead. They rode some more until the post came in sight: a long shack with a stable beside it.

'Now for the moment of truth,' Billy said.

'Just remember one thing.'

'What's that?'

'Keep it clammed.'

Close to, the shack looked to be all but falling down. A couple of shingles were missing from the roof, which was patched with tarpaper. The shutters hung askew from the windows. The gable boards were cracked and curling away from the stud frame. As they passed the stable a reek of dung and stale horse-sweat wafted from the open doors and somewhere in the dim interior a hound started up a hoarse barking.

'I'm surprised Wells Fargo gonna stand — '

'Shut up, damn it.'

They hitched their horses to the rail and pushed open the batwing doors. A bar ran along the back of the room and some tables and stools clustered round the stove and lined the side and front walls. A rank smell of old cooking grease came from the half-open door of the outhouse to the back of the bar. The door to the side room was shut.

Billy leaned down to the bar and blew a cloud of dust off the counter and over the row of glasses and couple of bottles that lined the back shelf.

The door of the side room creaked open.

'Was takin' a siesta,' a gravelly voice said.

The owner of the voice shuffled through the door drawing a suspender strap over a stained vest. He left the other to dangle and stood while he wiped some crust from his eye, examined it on his thumb for a moment, and wiped it on his greasy army pants. Then he hawked up a good wad of phlegm and let it droop into a spittoon beside the door. His arms were thick, too swollen in the biceps to hang straight by his side. His head was big as a medium-sized pumpkin and joined his shoulders without much sign of a neck. The features were big in proportion, with a nose like a fat pale strawberry, big rheumy brown eyes, and a mouth that didn't quite manage to keep the top front teeth covered. He never looked at them once, but waddled on his thick little stumps over behind the bar and let out a couple of ear-splitting coughs to show he wasn't to be messed with.

'You Carter?'

'No, I'm the Queen of the Fairies on my day off. Who you think I am?'

'I kind of thought you was Carter. My name's Stone and this here is my partner Caffrey.'

'Well, we don't see much custom and it takes me a while to get sociable. But lets have a drink while we're waiting. I got red-eye, red-eye, red-eye and rotgut — what'll it be.'

'Red-eye.'

'High damn, forgot we drunk the last of the red-eye — have to be rotgut.'

Carter poured whiskey into three dingy glasses.

'Good luck . . . Caffrey here's dumb, ain't he?'

Billy made a couple of passes in front

of his mouth and finished with a lip fart.

'How'd the job go?'

'Well enough. Had to kill a teller.'

'Damn bank clerks. Five-dollar-a-week heroes. Were you followed?'

'We shook them.'

'Hope so, otherwise I'll have to hide you in the hole under the livery stable. When's the rest of the boys coming?'

'Could be here any time. Depends how soon they can shake the rangers — they sent a ranger party out special looking for us. We just gonna wait here till the rest turn up.'

'Yeah, sure, I'll make you comfortable.'

'Mighty kind of you.'

'Don't worry about it. Wait till you see the bill. You done drunk ten dollars worth of whiskey already. I 'spect you're hungry. How about a nice twenty dollar supper?'

'What is it?'

'Mess of beans.'

'Beans come mighty expensive in these parts.'

'Five cents a bean. Don't worry, I'll throw you in some belly pork too.'

The rangers drank whisky to the sound of spitting grease from the outhouse as Carter cooked supper. Barnes was beginning to show the strain, and more than once Mike had to raise a finger to his lips as he looked about to try a whisper, whereupon Billy would make faces like a man heaving on a stuck cartwheel as he choked back the words.

They ate in the outhouse where the greasy boards gave off a sour reminder of old meals and nameless filth crusted the cooking stove and washtub, though at least the steam of cooking kept the dust caked in here.

As they spooned up their beans, Carter sawed on a grey loaf of half-risen bread.

'You want a little skillet grease spread on your bread? No? What's up with tongue-tied Daisy?'

Billy was flinging his hands around.

'He wants to tell you he'll cut his own.'

'It ain't no bother.'

Carter passed Mike a slice of bread that bore the indentation of his thumb in its doughy texture.

'I like it with a smear of skillet grease myself,' Carter said, slinging a dab of warm bacon fat on his bread and smoothing it flat. 'Makes it slide down juicy.'

He gobbled his food like a famished dog, pasting beans on his bread and jamming it into his mouth, pausing now and then to swig from a big tin mug, but not stopping to wipe the coffee trickles that ran over his chin. Every so often he would let loose a loud gurgling belch.

When the meal was finished, Carter pushed the table with its load of dirty plates over to the back wall of the outhouse, then opened up a folding card table between a bunk and a couple of stuffed chairs and plunked down a deck of cards.

'I don't use the bar much, it's more homey in here. Your friend OK to play?

He looks kinda sluggish in the brain department. I can't remember if they said he was touched. They said he was ugly. Weren't lyin'.'

Carter dealt cards, poured them whiskey in their coffee mugs and they settled down to play.

Mike felt Billy's elbow dig his arm.

'What's that?'

'What?'

'Heard something outside.'

Carter looked up from his cards.

'Oh, that. It'll be that runt prowlin' about. Don't pay no mind. Play.'

One of the outhouse doorsteps creaked.

Carter raised his head and bellowed, 'You prowlin', runt?'

Carter swapped a card, muttering, 'Goddam runt.'

Mike caught a glimpse of movement through the partly open outhouse door.

Carter sucked in a lungful of air and bellowed, 'What the hell you want?'

A child's voice spoke. 'Want some 'em 'er beans.'

'You can hightail it to hell's hallway. You goddam prowlin' little prairie rat.'

The kid's shadow moved, but he wasn't gone; a moment later his voice came again.

'You's finished with 'em beans. You's only gonna throw 'em to the dawg.'

Carter's big tombstones gleamed in the lamplight.

'I'd a'rather the hound had them than you. Now, vamoose.'

But the kid stayed put.

'Dawg's had his feed. I ain't eat all day.'

Mike thought Carter was going to make a spring for the door, but then his mouth widened in a grin and he winked at Mike.

'Goddammit, then come and get your stinkin' beans, then maybe you can get the hell away and leave a man play cards in peace.'

Bit by bit the outhouse door creaked open and the kid edged out of the shadows into the lamplight. He looked to be about six or seven. His cotton pants and shirt wouldn't survive a washing, and his hair probably washed fair but was now grey and stiff with dust. His legs were like sticks and his arms like twigs, and it looked like he'd gone barefoot a year at least. Crouching in the doorway, his eyes glanced uneasily between the dirty plates and Carter.

Keeping one eye on Carter, the kid edged his way from the doorway to the table. As he began to pick the few leftover beans off the plates, Carter snatched up his mug and flung it.

The big tin mug hit the boy square on the side of the head. But the boy didn't cry out or change expression, even stopped to snatch up one or two remaining beans and a crust of bread before darting for the door.

Carter whooped as the boy's black heels disappeared out the door.

'You'll see that tomorrow, you little pig's fart.'

Mike laid a hand on Billy's arm, narrowed his eyes in warning. When he felt Billy ease back he withdrew his hand.

'Hot damn, what a pure-dee beaut of a shot. Plumb square on the head-bone. You see that?'

'Was a pretty fair throw,' Mike agreed.

'Pretty fair. Hell, you hear that tin cup bong offa his h'yead? He'll have a goose egg sproutin' tomorrow, I guarantee it.'

'I'd say so. Who is he?'

'Ah, he's a runt got left here by a whore. His mama stayed here a while 'bout a year — nearly two year ago. I woke one mornin' and she'd upped and gone, left a note on the pillow saying she's headed to Abilene and when she'd made some money outa the US Cavalry there she'd come back and collect her son and pay for his back-keep too. That was nearly two years ago. I never 'spect to see her again. The kid does though. She told him she'd be back and he believed her. That's why he keeps a'hoverin' round here, like a damn fly round a jelly pot. I can't quite make up my mind to chase him off for good. His ma might come back, and I don't guess I'd get even a sniff of her ass if she found I'd run him off. Some of these whore bitches can be strange about their drop. I let him do some work and throw a few scraps to him ever' once in a while.'

5

Judging him by the state of the Staging Post and his person, Mike had put Carter down as idle to the bone, so it was surprising next day to see him sitting outside the stable on an upturned bucket heaving an anvil from the ground to his chin and back again.

'Like to keep my arms hard.' Carter curled his right arm. 'See this here arm? Ain't nobody gonna put this arm to the table. Was a champeen Indian wrestler in the army.'

'Abe taken a notion to ride into the hills and hunt,' Mike said.

'Sure. Tell you what, I'll saddle up old Dusty for him. Your mounts could do with some more resting up.'

As Carter went into the stable to fetch old Dusty, Billy hefted the anvil to try the weight. He nodded, impressed.

'Here she is. Dusty may not be so

fast, but she's a good old nag.'

Carter emerged trailing a grey mare that stood listlessly, blinking in the sunlight. He saddled her up and held her while Billy mounted. Billy gave a shake to the reins, but the mare wouldn't budge. Finally at a prod of the spurs, the mare neighed and rose high before it plunged down on its forelegs, back legs kicking at the sky. Dust rose in a cloud as the animal bucked and reared, and when the dust settled, it revealed Billy Barnes stretched out on his back.

Carter threw his hands wide. 'Don't know what got into that nag.' He seemed to be having trouble breathing, and finally had to turn away with shoulders shaking as he began wheezing like a locomotive leaking steam. Stamping his foot and shaking his head, he gasped, 'Oh, high damn,' and clamped his hand to his mouth to stifle his merriment.

Billy slowly picked himself up and glared at Carter's vibrating back as he began to advance. Mike raised a flat palm, shook his head, and Billy, snarling like a toothless wolf, turned and stalked back into the shack.

'You see that big monkey pitch off on his asshole?'

Mike laughed. 'Yeah, sure was comical the expression on his face, like somebody'd whacked him from behind with a fence-stake. Trouble with Abe though, he ain't got enough brains to have a sense of humour. He's mighty mad.'

'He don't worry me. Heard he was yeller. Though I admire the way he grilled that deputy. Heard about that too. I guess he hollered some, that old deputy?'

'Like to wake the dead.'

'I bet. Well, gonna take a look at my vegetable patch, see if that runt watered it.'

Mike headed back to the shack, and as he stepped through the door a hand grabbed his collar and he found himself nose to nose with Billy Barnes.

'I can't take much more of this,' Billy hissed.

Mike prised Billy's fist off his collar.

'Take it easy,' he whispered. 'You're doing fine. Carter don't suspect a thing. I'm proud of you, partner. I'm going to put you in for a mention.'

'If you so much let out a mutter 'bout this when we get back, I swear — '

'Calm down, Billy. Damnation, nobody said rangering was easy. And clam up, you never know when you could give yourself away.'

Billy spat and almost took the door off its hinges as he banged it after him.

Billy went over to the stable. He had nothing against the mare and figured the best way to ease his feelings was to try to make friends with it.

The animal gazed at him listlessly. Through the stable door, Billy spied Carter's head far off above some young corn stalks. He turned back to the mare and began to talk to it low and easy.

'Come on, girl, you didn't mean no

harm. What say we be friends? I don't reckon you're mean tempered, I reckon you just don't cotton to a big gorilla like me squatting on your backbone. Can't say I blame you. I believe you're a good old girl at heart, but less I'm mistaken you ain't feelin' too good. Your eyes ain't as bright as they could be, and I speculate y'all got a low fever. I bet your blood's just hummin', ain't it? And hey, just look at that big old boil under your haunch. I bet that pains you some. C'mere girl.'

The mare kept its sick eyes on Billy all the while he talked and finally it responded to his beckoning hand and shuffled over.

'There now. That's a good girl.'

Billy led the mare out of its stall and moving along its flank, patting it all the time, he bent to examine the boil.

'That boil's ripe and tender. You just take it easy and I'm gonna fix it for you.'

Billy slipped out his pocket knife and opened a blade. The horse barely quivered at the quick slash. It turned its head round to look as the puss ran down its leg.

'There . . . bet that feels easier,' Billy whispered. 'Now, just you hold your hosses there and don't go 'way for one itty-bitty second . . . reason for why — I got sumpin' I b'lieve you gon' like.'

Billy went to his saddle-bags that hung on the rail of one of the stalls and fished out a bundle of greased paper. He went over to the bench that ran along the back wall and sat and opened the paper bundle beside him. He picked a good-sized sugar chip from the bundle and held it out in the palm of his hand. The mare came over, had a sniff and a lick, and finding it was good, began to eat.

Billy tensed. He could have sworn he'd heard a rustle of movement. It had seemed to come from low down over in the far corner of the stable.

He peered into the shadows, but could see nothing. After a while, he picked out another chip of the sugar loaf and went back to feeding the mare.

Out of the corner of his eye he saw the kid sidling along the wall. Billy didn't turn his head, just continued feeding the mare sugar. Finally the kid's head poked out from behind the mare's haunch. Billy gave him one glance, then turned his attention to the mare again. When the kid plucked up courage, he came and stood before Billy with his eyes fixed on the paper bundle full of sugar lumps.

Without looking at the kid, Billy picked out a lump and held it out on his palm. The kid was as wary as the mare, but the sight of the sugar proved too tempting. He came closer, and when he was close enough reached out a filthy paw for the lump.

At that moment Billy looked up and spotted Carter heading back up towards the shack. An alarm sounded in his brain. The kid knew he could speak, and he had an idea that if he made friends with him the kid might rouse Carter's suspicions by trying to talk to him.

All at once, instead of gazing at the sugar lump, the kid found he was staring at Billy's closed fist.

Billy read the hurt in the kid's eyes. The next instant he read the look that said he might have known better, was only fooled by the kind way Billy had spoken to the mare. Then the kid's dirt-caked feet were pounding dust as he disappeared out the door of the livery.

Billy sat and showed his bare gums and glared at Carter's pumpkin head as he rolled up out of the vegetable patch.

6

Carl Johansson cooked dinner and laid it on an old washboard by way of a tray. It was a good supper of beefsteaks and fried potatoes, because no matter what those men in his root cellar had done, they were still human beings after all and he wasn't going to feed them as if they were dogs.

Carl used a napkin to lift a pot of hot coffee off the stove and adding a good-sized hunk of bread to the tray he carried it out to the front of the house. He laid the tray down by the cellar trap, with a napkin over it to keep off the dust, and then he went back inside the house to fetch his shotgun out from the corner of the chimney-breast where he kept it hidden. He didn't like to keep a gun in sight, much less hanging on the wall, because he didn't like guns and regretted the necessity for killing, as he regretted the necessity for dying, and all those other harsh facts of existence that now, after sixty-seven years, seemed only harsher than ever.

As he bent to draw the bar on the trap door he heard a muffled sound coming from the cellar. It was very much like someone moaning. One of those men was wounded. The rangers had said it was nothing to worry about, and it hadn't looked very serious to Carl either, but they weren't doctors, and the wounded man certainly sounded in a bad way.

Carl threw up the trap and stood back.

'You can come up now and get your dinner. I'll fix you some beefsteaks.'

The moaning came loud and clear out of the open hatch. The man couldn't shout or cuss or explain how bad he felt, and his moaning had the forlorn sound of a dumb animal that understands nothing except that it hurts and is weak and sick.

The blond man's head rose out of the

hatch and he blinked helplessly as he looked round for Carl.

'My partner's awful sick,' the blond man said. He stood there with only his head and shoulders showing above the ground, his face screwed up against the sun's glare. 'I sat up with him all night, and held his hand while he tossed and turned and moaned. My own hand aches with how he been clutchin' at it when the spasms gripped him, but I couldn't refuse to give him my hand, because we been partners a long time, and it seemed the only thing that brought him some comfort in his agony.'

'He sound bad, all right,' Carl said.

'He is, mister, he's awful bad. I don't believe his time is long now. Fifteen years we rid the range together, since we was just green boys. We neither of us have no family, no wives or sweethearts, so we been brothers each to the other, and much as I'd miss old Abe, if I'd a gun I reckon I'd put a bullet in his brain myself the way you'd show mercy to a sufferin' animal.'

'You better come get your dinner.'

Carl watched him as he climbed out of the cellar and went to pick up the tray. He supposed outlaws looked about the same as other men. This one looked liked a decent German boy. They called him Stone; in the Old Country it was probably Stein. He had the same thick northern blood in his veins as Carl. His own eldest son would have been about the same age if he'd lived. He would have had the same colour hair and eyes too. Blue skies over wheat fields, his wife Ingrid used to call it. The other had an Irish look. When first he came to the new country, he'd worked on the railway among a gang of Irish boys. They always had a song and a joke and a friendly word and could work like mules the day long.

'Your friend — '

The blond stopped halfway down the hatch and turned back to look at Carl.

'Can he walk?'

'I reckon he can still walk, just about.'

'You send him up.'

'All right, I will. Thank you, mister. Thank you, and God bless you.'

A few moments later, the mute began to clamber out of the hatch.

'I want that you stay there,' Carl told the blond. 'I go lock you in. Got to be careful.'

'Sure, that's OK. I'll stay here. I'll be mighty thankful if you can ease my partner any.'

The wounded man looked unsteady on his feet, but Carl didn't take any chances, he kept him covered with the shotgun while he stumbled to the screen door.

'There, now, you doing fine, son,' Carl said. 'Jus' you try make it over to the couch.'

The man careened across the room and collapsed on the couch. Carl fetched his shaving razor from the kitchen, laid the gun against the wall and cut away the man's sleeve.

The man lay with his eyes closed, moving his head from side to side and moaning weakly.

'It's swelled up little bit . . . don't think got gangrene . . . '

The mute's eyes opened. Carl gazed into the brown-flecked green pupils.

The mute's hand shot up and grabbed Carl's throat. Carl gagged. The mute's fingers and thumb dug into his throat either side of his Adam's apple and he felt his eyes bulge. He reached for the shotgun leaning against the wall, but the mute swung himself upright and flung him across the room. When Carl hauled himself off the wreckage of a straight-backed chair the mute had his shotgun in his hands and Carl was gazing down the barrels of it.

Motioning him outside, the mute ordered him with grunts and gestures of the shotgun to unbar the cellar hatch.

The blond came up the cellar stairs with a half-eaten beefsteak in his hand. He tore off a bite and as he chewed said, 'Get in the house.'

'What are you going — '

Carl's ear rang to a swipe of the blond's open hand.

'Are you deaf?'

The mute trotted Carl to the house prodding him in the buttocks with the shotgun as he went.

Stone tore another chunk off the beefsteak and tossed it into the corner of the room, wiping his hand on his shirt as he chewed.

'You got any other weapons, Swede?'

'A Remington handgun and a Winchester rifle, I got, that's all.'

'Well, what're you waitin' for?'

Carl turned and headed for the bedroom where he kept the weapons.

'Hey,' Stone barked. 'C'mere.'

Carl came back and stood in front of him.

'Where you think you're lopin' off to?'

'I tink you want me fetch guns.'

'You *tink* . . . .' Stone warmed Carl's other ear with a head-rocking slap. 'You *tink* I'm gonna let you go in there and come out blazin' with your arsenal? Take Abe with you, you stupid Swede.'

Carl made for the door again, but stopped when Caffrey didn't follow him.

'What're you waitin' for?'

'He not come — '

Stone gritted his teeth. 'Goddam, Swede, you like vexin' me?'

Carl gave a little tug at the mute's sleeve. With a growl, Caffrey swung the shotgun and laid the barrels across Carl's face.

Carl lay on the floor. His cheekbone was broken and his mouth was full of blood. He was afraid to get up, and afraid to lie there, in case by lying there he made them angry. He closed his eyes and lay still, hoping they would think he was unconscious. But the fear was worse when he couldn't see and he couldn't keep his eyelids from twitching, so he opened his eyes again.

Stone gave a couple of short sharp whistles.

'Up, Swede. Up, boy. Up on your hind legs.'

Carl struggled to his feet.

'Why you boys don't shoot me and have done?'

But this was a mistake. They didn't like him acting brave. Caffrey ran at him and swung the shotgun, slamming the butt down on his foot. The shotgun went off blasting a hole in the pine boards of the ceiling. Dust and woodchips rained down while Carl hopped on one foot, his ears ringing. He saw Caffrey shake his head, and heard, as if from a long way away, Stone laughing and saying, 'You done made yourself deaf as well as dumb, Abe.'

They didn't like him looking at them either, so Carl kept his eyes down. He had to call Stone 'sir' when he spoke to him. They had him make coffee and spat it in his face because it wasn't to their liking. Carl felt sick. He felt like he could vomit at any minute. His heart was racing and would stop beating for seconds at a time. His vision would darken while the blood whistled in his ears, but the dark waves would recede without him losing consciousness.

The mute was playing with his razor, and Carl felt a terrible weakness run all through his body at the sight of the mute's brutish green eyes.

'What's that, Abe?'

The mute did a little shuffle on the floor and honked his jarring laugh.

'Yeah, that's right,' said Stone. 'Abe says dance, Swede.'

Sixty-seven years old, Carl thought. My dancing days are over. He thought of his wife watching him from somewhere, except he'd never been sure there was a somewhere to watch from.

'Dance.'

Caffrey pretended to play some kind of demented honking fiddle, and they kept ordering him to dance, but he wouldn't dance, so they kept hurting him. It wasn't the hurting so much . . . it wasn't the fear so much . . . he'd suffered pain and fear before . . . but there'd always been an end to it. This didn't stop and it was wearing him down. He remembered a schoolmaster reading what some old Roman general had said to his troops before some ancient battle, how he'd told them that few men were born naturally brave, but through discipline and practice they could learn to act bravely. He'd thought that Roman general was wise and knew men. He'd always tried to be brave in his life, though he regretted the need for it, and didn't see it as the be-all and end-all as they did in these wild parts . . . but now he was tired of being brave, couldn't see much use in it after all. It was only pride, and no one was watching, or if anyone was watching from somewhere else . . . if there was a somewhere else to watch from . . . then they should understand.

Carl began to dance.

Caffrey encouraged him with the razor, and when he was finished, Stone blew his head off with both barrels.

7

'I do the damned cookin' round here.'

Carter's fat nose twitched.

'What's that smell?'

Billy opened the oven door and pulled out a tray and the aroma of new-baked bread banished the stink of Carter's outhouse.

'Who tol' you you could make them biscuits?'

Billy mimed counting out money into Carter's hands.

'You betcha you'll pay for it. Let's see . . . Hey, what's this?' Carter peeled off one of two thick slices of bacon that flanked a mound of grits on a tin platter. 'This cost you twenty-fi' dollars at least.'

Billy almost nodded his head off his shoulders to indicate it was OK. He made gestures to explain that after the sun rose twice more and Tindale came with the money, he would pay Carter fifty dollars for his meal. Billy was discovering he was good at sign language. He guessed he was just a born communicator, and whether it was a question of regular speaking or mute-talk, his natural talent was bound to shine through.

'I be makin' supper in a couple of hours. I don't know why'all you caint wait.'

That was OK, Billy mimed; this was just a snack, and he would be ready to eat again at supper time.

'Well, it's up to you. I was fixin' to cook warmed-over jerky and rice, too.'

Billy picked up his piled plate and balanced the bread on top.

I'm going outside to eat my meal under the shade of the trees, Billy mimed one-handed.

'Now where the hell you goin'?' Carter demanded as Billy headed out the back door, ' . . . like a damn animal, fixin' to eat his grub under God's open sky.'

Platter in hand, Billy wandered down through the vegetable patch, then made a circuit of the staging post. Among the weeds at the side of the stable he glimpsed a movement. He headed towards it and saw the weeds rustle as if some small animal had taken fright and made its escape towards the back of the stable. Billy doubled back to the other side of the stable and stood waiting at the corner. He heard the kid come rustling through the weeds and when he appeared at the corner, Billy reached down and grabbed a handful of shirt collar. The kid took off back the way he'd come and Billy followed, letting him have his head. The rotten material of the kid's shirt shredded, but the front seam held, and when they reached the back of the stable, Billy hauled back and the kid came down on his hindquarters.

'Hol' up, old hoss,' Billy said, keeping his voice low.

The kid sat against the stable wall

with his head down, breathing fast, his chest heaving.

'I threw a scare into you in the barn there a while back,' Billy said. 'I seed ol' melon-head comin' up out of the corn-patch and got rattled. I didn't want him thinkin' I was friendly with you. Was a stupid idea, but I never was good at thinkin' fast. He don't know I can talk, but now you do, so when I got to thinkin' it over proper I decided best thing is for us to join forces 'gainst that ol' buzzard. What's your opinion on it?'

The kid used a grimy hand to scratch some burrs out of his tangle of hair and also to hide his face behind. Otherwise, he sat as before: head down and chest heaving.

'I guess you don't like to gab, do you? You and my partner Mike would get on. Say, you peckish?'

Billy laid the tin platter at the kid's feet. The kid stared at it but made no move towards it.

'Now, don't you go takin' off.' Billy eased his hand off the kid's collar and sat back against the stable boards.

Somewhere out in the sage, the hound set up a barking and scared a trio of crows into flight. Billy took out his pocketknife and started shaving a splinter he prised off a rotten board.

'I don't blame you turnin' up your nose at that grub. The grits ain't too bad — I make good grits, but I never could get the biscuits just right. My ma, now, she made the best biscuits I ever tasted. God rest her. She's dead now — fell down a well five or eight years ago. Drewed up that bucket and there was ma, stone drowned. Hell, maybe that hound could stand some grits. I reckon I'll go and see.' Billy picked up the platter and brought it under the kid's nose. 'You sure you won't try a piece of that bacon on a biscuit?'

The kid reached out a hand and picked up a biscuit.

'That's the style.' Billy knifed one of the bacon slices and slung it on the kid's biscuit.

The first couple of bites were slow

and reluctant, as if the taste of the food made the kid a little sick, but before long he'd found his stride and he couldn't get that food off the tin plate fast enough, shovelling handfuls of grits in, gnawing off lumps of bacon and trying to wedge it into a mouth already choked with bread.

'I'm right glad you appreciate my cookin'. 'Course, you might be just bein' polite.'

Billy waited till the kid was reduced to searching lone grits that had escaped him and said, 'Say, what's your name anyway?'

The kid pretended to pick burrs out of his hair, but behind his hand Billy suspected he was nerving himself to speak.

'It's Billy,' the kid said in a rusty voice.

'By . . . I don' . . . oh, hell, you ain't even har'ly gonna *believe* what I'm gonna tell you. Do you know what my name is? Why, my name, sir, my name is Billy too. I swear it by my hoss's toes.'

'Hoss ain't got no toes. Got hoofs.'

Billy pounded his knee hard enough to raise dust. He snatched off his hat, jammed it back on his head, thrust his face at the kid and cried, 'By' — Billy caught himself, brought his voice down to a fierce whisper — 'damn . . . I knowed it. I said to my partner Mike when I seed you, 'I got a suspicion that kid's smart'. And I was right, damn it. How many kids your age know you call what a hoss got hoofs? Well, I'd just like to know, sir, 'cause I'd bet my ranger's pay there ain't many.'

'That were easy.'

'Well, sir, it might be easy fer you . . . '

'Are you a ranger?'

'Now how in the hungry heckus did you know that?'

'You jist said it. You jist said, I bet my ranger's pay.'

'Listen, I'm gonna call you Little Billy, OK? Little Billy, I'm a Texas Ranger, it's true, but if you breathe a word of it to anybody my life won't be

71

worth a Dixie dollar. Are you gonna keep my secret, or are you gonna blab and get me killed?'

'I won't. The man can whup me with his ol' hickory stick too, but I won't tell.'

'He whups you with his ol' hickory stick, huh?'

'I declare it.'

'Well, won't be many more whuppins with that ol stick. You just hol' tough and I'll see you right, Little Billy.'

'You gonna 'rest the man?'

'You want me to arrest him?'

'Yeah, I guess so.'

'Well, I'll do it. But we got to wait a spell. His friends are comin' soon, maybe tomorrow, and when they get here, me and my partner Mike, we'll arrest them and ol' melon-head too. In the meantime the man got to think I'm a bad man. He thinks my name is Abe and I'm a mute. You know what mute is?'

'I think so . . . '

'It means dumb, can't talk. So don't

you fret if I don't talk to you none, 'cause I'll just be pretendin', to fool the man. And I want you to pretend that me and my partner are bad men just like the man and you gotta let on to be scared of us. Can you do that?'

'That's easy.'

'It only looks like it's easy 'cause you're a smart kid.'

They heard a rustling and the dog came trotting out of the weeds and began nosing at the bacon grease on the tin platter. Billy glanced over and saw the boy's face for the first time full on. He guessed the purple bruise on his temple was from when Carter shied the cup at him. The kid's eyes were following Billy's knife as it took shavings off the strip of board.

Billy folded the knife blade back into its deer-horn handle and held it out to the boy.

'Keep it.'

'Golly,' the kid breathed.

'But don't you let ol' melon-head see that knife, you hear? You keep it well hid.' The kid gazed at the horn handle in his hand.

'This prob'ly the best knife I ever had, an' ol' melon-head ain't goin' see it neither.'

8

Mike was trying to worry and not look like he was worrying in case Carter wondered what he was worrying about. Tindale and his friend would likely be here tomorrow and it was up to him to think of every eventuality in order to avoid getting himself and Billy killed.

'You ready for another?'

'Not just yet.'

Carter grinned as he poured himself another shot, pleased with the fact that he'd already drunk three to Mike's one.

'You ain't much of a drinker then?' Carter downed his own and let out a sigh of relish.

'I generally drink a bottle a day, but I can't seem to stomach this stuff.'

'I generally drink two bottles a day.'

'What, this horse piss?'

'Well, I don' even care for that there bonded liquor. Tastes like cow milk to me. Least with this stuff a man can feel it going down.'

'When you expecting the next stage through here?'

'Oh, won't be till the start of next month. Wells Fargo don't use this route much now since the silver played out up in Vulture Gulch. If I'd to scratch a livin' out of this I'd be in a sorry fix. But this is just pin money to me. Dan Tindale ain't the only one I work with. 'Bout every six months Clyde Lavery will ride down out of Arkansas with a herd of rustled horses and I'll sell them for him — got contacts on the coast for that. Then there's Slim Sims — work with him too. Me and Dan goes back a long way though. You know Dan's kid brother — what was his name again . . . ?'

'Frederick.'

'Frederick, well he — no, are you sure?'

'I think it was Frederick. Dan don't mention him much now.'

'Why, what happened between them — they was close as could be?'

Mike scratched his jaw.

'Well, I tell you . . . I'd rather let Dan explain to you about that,' Mike said, and gave Carter a wink.

Carter's whiskey stopped halfway to his lips, his eyes widened, then narrowed, then widened again. 'Oh . . . yeah . . . Yeah, but — '

Mike heaved an impatient sigh and getting up off the barstool walked to the window.

'I was only going to say . . . oh, well, it don't matter.'

'You sure your calendar's right?' Mike said, looking out the window.

'Huh?'

'Got a stage coming.'

Carter strode over to the window.

'No goddam stage due till next month.'

But he couldn't deny the evidence of his eyes. A stage was raising a cloud of dust among the sage. Carter hurried out to meet it as it pulled up outside.

'What the hell's goin' on? You come here ten days ahead of schedule and I 'spose I got to fix you supper? Well supper gonna cost, I'll tell you that.'

Carter could keep his supper, the lone driver told him; all he wanted was a change of horse and he'd be on his way. The stage was a special charter: one passenger had wanted to travel and the company had a load of schoolbooks overdue for delivery up to Coolwater county, so they'd done a deal. Now, if Carter could change the team and pay the passenger's fare —

'Pay what?'

'Passenger said you'd pay the fare.'

Carter scuttled over and wrenched open the stage door.

'Milly.'

'Hello, Hank.'

A girl of about twenty-three or four stepped out of the stage. She was small but nicely curved, with a heart-shaped face framed by hair of silky light brown that was fixed in two side buns.

'You just gonna turn up here out of the blue, and naturally first thing I got to do is pay for your ride. Well, some things don't — I say some things sure don't change.'

'I'll pay you back, Hank.'

'Damn right you will,' Carter snickered.

'Can I have my property?' the girl said to the stage driver.

'Oh, near forgot.' The driver fished in his pocket. 'She gave me this to hold as surety for the fare.'

'Let me see that.' Carter snatched a necklace out of the driver's hand and examined it.

'I'll be able to pay you back out of that,' Milly said.

'Hmmph,' Carter growled.

The girl stopped inside the doorway when she saw Mike, then she dropped her eyes and nodded and, taking a seat by the bar, sat smiling at her hands folded in her lap. As soon as the team was changed and the driver paid, the stage pulled away and Carter bustled back inside.

'Where's Billy?' the girl said.

'Oh, he's around somewheres,' Carter

said as he dumped her travelling grip down by the side of the bar.

'Will you call him, Hank?'

'Hold your horses. Have a drink first. If you was so all-fired anxious to see him, you could've come before this. It's been a year-and-a-half at least. Take a drink.'

The girl blinked at the taste of the rotgut, but she didn't gag, and she put it away without much more trouble.

On second thoughts, Mike decided, she was closer to twenty-eight than twenty-four. She wasn't a stranger to the bottle, and it showed in her complexion which was a little mottled round the cheekbones. She was pretty enough, but she had been prettier, and there was something in her smile — a touch of regret — that seemed to show she knew it.

'I'm glad Billy's OK. I was worried about him.'

'Oh, yeah, well what kept you away so long?'

'I had some awful bad luck, Hank.

You don't know the times I had this last year. I took sick with the pleurisy, then I been in the female penitentiary — '

'Oh, yeah? Where'd you get that necklace?'

'It belonged to a Methodist minister — or his wife, I should say. He took an interest in me and said he was going to save my soul. But it wasn't my soul he was interested in. He brought me to his house one night when his wife was away visiting, and told me he wanted to do it on their marriage bed. His wife had all kinds of lovely things, clothes and such — her family was well-to-do. I asked him if I could try on her necklace, and that was all right by him — he wanted me to wear her bonnet and shoes too. When he wasn't looking I sneaked out the door with the necklace. He used to spout the good book, but there wasn't an ounce of Christian charity in him. He took advantage of me being broke and having no one to turn to. So I paid him back, I guess. I hated that old man, and I had to get away from him, but I just didn't know where to go. Then one day, one of the other girls in this house for fallen women brought in a news rag that said how Danny had escaped from jail. It was a couple of days after that that I took off with the necklace and headed down to El Paso because I knew Danny's friends were there and I figured he'd show up there sooner or later. I never met Danny, but one day I bumped into little Felipe and he told me how he'd taken a message from Danny to you about some business in Stanhope, how they were going to take the bank and then bring the goods to you to fence. So as soon as I heard that, I got on the stage and came here straight away. I hope I'm not too late.'

'No, you ain't too late.'

'When's Danny coming?'

'Maybe tomorrow.'

'I ain't seen Danny in such a long time. Has he changed?'

'How the hell should I know, I ain't seen him in a coon's age either.'

The door opened and Billy came in.

He gave the girl a good looking-over.

'Hello,' Milly said.

Billy nodded and strode up to the bar and mimed that he could use a drink.

'I hope Billy's been good.'

Billy's head shot round.

'Have you seen Billy?' the girl asked, a little surprised at Billy's reaction.

'He's a mute,' Carter said. 'These are two of Dan's gang — Tom Stone and Abe Caffrey.'

Milly's eyes lit up. 'You know Danny?'

'Yeah,' Mike said. 'We helped him pull the job in Stanhope.'

'Is Danny all right? Did he get away safe? What does he mean . . . ? I don't understand . . . '

Billy was doing some hand waving. Most of it was taking place down about knee height.

'I believe he's talking about the kid,' Mike said.

Carter tapped Billy on the shoulder and stuck his face into Billy's, bellowing:

'YOU — MEAN — KID? WHAT — YOU — TRY — SAY?'

'Henry, call Billy for me . . . would you . . . please?'

Without much in the way of good grace, Carter nevertheless pushed out through the batwings and stood on the porch and hollered:

'RUNT. GET UP HERE, RUNT.'

Carter came back inside and poured the girl another drink, which she did not refuse.

'Can you let me have some money for the necklace?' the girl said.

'Now, what do you want money for? You never had any money last time you was here, and we got on just fine.'

One of the batwings creaked open. The boy dragged his bare feet reluctantly through the doorway.

The kid gazed at the woman, his grey eyes round under the tangle of dusty hair.

'Won't you say hello to mama?'

The kid rushed over and flung his arms out.

'Billy.'

The boy stopped before the girl's warding hand.

'Oh, sweetheart, look at you. You'll muss my dress, and it's the only one I got. You wait until you get cleaned up and mama will give you a big hug. Hank, just look at him. He's skinny as a fence picket.'

'Goddam it, you just left him on me. You're lucky I didn't run him off. What do I know about lookin' after kids?'

'Is that really my little Billy under all that dirt? Is it?'

The boy nodded. 'Yes, mama.'

'Oh, honeybunch . . . Did you miss mama?'

The boy gazed at her feet and nodded.

'Oh, Hank, have you been feeding him right? Do you want something to eat, Billy?'

'No.'

'Aren't you hungry?'

'I done et.'

'See,' Carter said. 'He ain't even

hungry, that proves he been getting fed at least. And you ain't even thanked me for taking care of that boy all this time.'

The girl stood up and went to her bag. She fished out a handkerchief with a bedraggled lace trim and coming back, moistened the handkerchief with her saliva, then bending over the boy, began to wipe his face.

'My, you're one dirty little boy,' she said as she wiped streaks in the grime. 'Don't you have a smile for mama?'

The boy stuck his knuckles in his eyes as they filled with tears.

'Oh, Billy, I missed you so.'

Carter, eyeing the girl's bustle that stuck up as she bent over the boy, tiptoed across the room. He stooped and raised the hem of the dress with a sly finger, and while the girl was still oblivious, stuck his arm under it.

'And I missed this.'

The girl shot upright.

'Hank.'

'Just checkin' it's still there.' Carter's laughter rattled the bottles behind the bar. Seeing Billy was about to make a club of a whiskey bottle, Mike slipped it out of his hand and gave him a look from under his brows.

Samson's face might have worn a like expression while he strained at the temple pillars, but under Mike's warning stare, Billy did no more than toss back the glass that Mike poured him.

9

The girl's presence encouraged Carter to bellow twice as loud and drink twice as fast as normal. His big pumpkin head glowed with whiskey and excitement, and though he left Mike pretty much alone, he couldn't resist trying to impress the girl by riding Billy.

'Ol' Gabby Gus there don't have much luck with the ladies I'm afraid, Milly. I introduced him to a sweet little filly yesterday, and she took agin' him right on the spot. Tricked him into mounting this here bucking mare and she took and gave a twitch of her back and next thing you'd a thunk you was watchin' one of them trapeze artists in a circus show way he sailed through the air.' Carter hee-heed and hawhawed till the bar-room shook. 'Oh, look, he's sulkin'. Hey, Gus, I was only funnin'. C'mere, let's be friends. Tell you what, how about a little friendly arm-wrestlin'?'

Carter hauled Billy over to one of the tables and plunked him down at it. He rested his elbow on it, grabbed Billy's arm and positioned it next to his.

Billy winced at the touch of Carter's moist palm. Carter began to heave and Billy pushed back. The grin on Carter's face turned to a snarl as he settled to some serious effort. His colour deepened and his eyes bulged. His head almost seemed to expand with the effort till it made Billy think of a big red over-ripe melon about to pop its rind.

Billy locked his shoulder tight and pushed with the flat slabs of muscle on his back. Carter's arm strained the cotton of his vest. His chin sank further into his chest and his shoulders rose till they nudged his ears. A trickle of sweat oozed down his forehead.

Billy locked his eyes on Carter's and called up an extra bit of effort. He saw the sudden vulnerability in Carter's eyes before his arm began to bend back.

Carter's hand moved backwards two inches then stopped. He showed Billy the top of his head and from his throat came a sound like a big file slowly grinding. Bit by bit, Carter's hand began to come upright. His head came up and his eyes bored into Billy's, full of triumph. His tombstone teeth glistened as they bit down on his lower lip. Billy's hand began to move backwards.

Billy caught Mike's eye. Mike raised his glass, thought better of it, and laid it down again. The girl was watching Carter, the boy's eyes were fixed on Billy.

Billy locked up his shoulder again and hauled the power up out of his back muscles. Carter's hand shook and his fat cheeks trembled with effort, but his arm moved inexorably backwards. Inch by inch it moved past the upright. Then Billy eased off the power and Carter's eyes blazed once more as he pushed Billy back.

Billy let Carter push him back six

more times. Each time, Carter felt victory in his teeth, and though sustained effort was not in his nature, he called up reserves of strength he didn't know he had.

Mike made a sign to him, an almost imperceptible shake of the head to Billy and a nod at Carter's straining back. That suited Billy's humour too: he could have put Carter's hand right through the table, but since he was in the business of fooling Carter it seemed extra sly to let Abe Caffrey lose this little contest.

Carter wheezed and gasped. He could hardly believe that victory was six more inches away; he couldn't understand how he'd found the strength left after all that effort to bring it so close. But, with the eyes of the girl on him, he found somewhere in the depths of his being something that was almost heroic, something that, whatever it was, was just enough to finally flatten the mute's hand against the table.

Carter slumped back in his seat. He

couldn't even feel his arm. There was a flecked mist in front of his eyes.

'I guess I deserve a drink after that,' he panted.

Carter went to the bar, picked up the whiskey bottle and poured whiskey all over the counter. He found he had to grab the bottle by both hands before he could direct any liquor into the glass.

Billy discovered the boy's eyes on him. The boy hung his head, and unnoticed by his mother who was attending to Carter's ranting, dragged his feet out through the batwing doors.

Billy stood up and followed the kid out behind the stable.

'Hey, you think I couldn't beat ol' melon-head if I wanted to?'

'I guess you could,' the kid said politely.

'That was Abe Caffrey wrestlin'. Why I'm famous as Herc'cles as a strongman — if ol' Abe had a rep that way, most like it would've got about.'

Now the kid probably just thought he was a blow-hard in the bargain.

'Yeah, you think I'm just makin' excuses. I wished I had beat him now. But ol' melon-head will be easier to handle now he's all puffed up and full of hisself. There's two ways to win the affection of a guy like that. You can beat him down and he'll end up fawnin' over you like a puppy dog — but he'll love you even more if he thinks he can beat you down. He's gonna keep on treatin' me like dirt, but it'll kind of tickle him that I make him look good. We got to keep ol' melon-headed tickled and struttin' like a rooster, and that way he won't start mopin' and thinkin' and 'fore you know getting suspicious.'

'He's gonna look silly when he finds out you're a Texas Ranger, I guess. I bet he just falls right over on the ground when he finds out.'

'He'll probably fall right down in a dead faint. Let's go back inside.'

The kid turned the corner of the stable and Billy heard him gasp. The kid reappeared, a handful of his hair in Tom Stone's fist. The mute came behind with a shotgun levelled at Billy's chest.

'How you been keeping, Ranger?' Stone said. 'We got fed up with that Swede's company, so we thought we'd look you up.'

The mute kept giving Billy painful jabs in the spine with the shotgun and when they reached the shack he gave him a shove in the ass with his boot that sent him crashing through the batwing doors.

'Billy,' the girl cried. 'Leave him alone.'

Stone let go of the kid's hair and the kid backed over to the wall where he stood head down, staring up at Stone and Caffrey.

'We ain't got no money,' Carter said. 'You boys is wastin' your time.'

'You Carter?' Stone said.

'That's right. Henry Carter. You can take what I got, but I only got a few dollars. I don't know what these others got.'

'We're with Dan Tindale. I'm Tom Stone and this is Abe Caffrey.' Stone looked at Mike. 'You waitin' to be asked politely?'

Mike unbuckled his gun belt and Billy did the same.

'If you're Stone and Caffrey, who are these?'

'They're Texas Rangers.'

'Texas Rangers?' Carter breathed.

'I don't know who the Texas Rangers are but it ain't us,' Mike said.

'You oughtn't to lie when you're about to meet your Maker.'

'We'll see who the liar is when Dan gets here,' Mike said.

Carter looked from Mike to Stone.

Stone raised his Winchester and aimed it at the middle of Mike's head.

'The smoke of my gun's the last thing you'll see.'

'Wait,' Carter cried. 'I don't want to have to clean a ton of blood and slime offa here. You can take 'em outside. But first of all, why don't you boys have a drink?'

Carter found a couple of glasses and poured whiskey. He gave one to Stone then scuttled over to Caffrey and said, 'Here, gimme that gun. You go and have yourself a drink, I'll keep these two covered.'

Caffrey handed over the shotgun and went over to join Stone at the bar.

'Help yourself to another.'

As Caffrey poured more drinks, Carter edged closer to the bar. Stone raised his glass and as he tipped it to his lips, Carter jammed the shotgun in his back.

'OK, drop that Winchester.'

Stone let the rifle clatter to the floor.

'What's the idea?' Stone said.

'Good work,' Mike said as he strode across and bent to pick up the Winchester.

Carter pointed the shotgun at him.

'Back off.'

'What's the matter with you?' Mike said.

'I don't know who the hell anybody is,' Carter said. 'So when Dan Tindale gets here, he can sort you out.'

10

Carter sent the girl out to watch for Tindale, then stationed himself behind the bar with the shotgun in his hands, ready to swivel it to cover either Caffrey and Stone who sat to the right of the bar, or Mike and Billy to the left.

Swinging the barrels to Stone, he said, 'What colour eyes Dan got?'

'What colour eyes?' Stone frowned.

'Don't you know?'

'They ain't brown or dark-coloured . . . Blue.'

'So Dan Tindale's got blue eyes? I think I'll blast you right now.'

'Wait, slow down, dammit. I never paid no attention to his eyes.' Then shooting a finger at Mike, 'Does he know?'

'Grey eyes,' Mike said. 'Dan's got grey eyes. Why don't you open that son-of-a-bitch up?'

'He could've got that from a description. He's a ranger. He'll have posters and descriptions and all kinds of information on outlaws.' Stone's hand shot up. 'Wait, Dan's got a scar.'

'That's right enough,' Carter said. 'Got a long scar on his thigh where a tree splinter tore him open at Bull Run.'

'Goddam it,' Stone yelped. 'He mightn't have knowed that.'

'Which thigh is it on, Ranger?' Mike said to Stone.

'Why the hell don't *you* tell me?'

'If you're Tom Stone, you should know,' Mike said.

'Hellfire and damnation . . . I do know.'

Carter's pumpkin head turned from one to the other. His tongue poked between his tombstone teeth.

'I guess you just don't feel like saying . . . Carter.'

Carter's head swivelled to face Mike. 'Huh?'

'Blow his lying head off.'

Carter half-raised the shotgun.

'Wait . . . dammit . . . wait. Wait till Tindale gets here. I ain't afraid.'

'He's playing for time.'

There was a rattle on the boards outside and the girl sent the batwings swinging, running in.

'Someone's coming. Two riders. I think one of them's Dan.'

She began to fluff up the ruffles on her dress and pinch her cheeks. After jittering about some more, she collected herself and walked slowly to the corner of the bar where she took a seat and bent her head to sit smiling at her hands.

The drum of hoofs grew louder. Somewhere out by the stable horses were reined to a halt, a confused clatter of feet made the boards vibrate, and two men, one supporting the other, lurched through the batwing doors.

'Gimme a hand, boys,' the tall, fair-haired man called out, 'Waco's hurt.'

Stone and Caffrey rushed to help the man with the bloodstained shirt to a chair.

'What's up?' The fair-haired man stood hands on hips in the middle of the room and took in the shotgun in Carter's hands and then, narrowing his eyes at Mike and Billy, said, 'Who's this?'

'They's a couple of rangers, Dan,' Stone said.

'Rangers, you say?'

'Hello, Danny.'

At the sound of the girl's voice, Tindale spun round.

The girl blushed under Tindale's piercing stare, then she smiled and said, 'Don't you remember me?'

'Seems I might.'

'Milly,' the girl prompted.

'Why, sure, Milly . . . what the hell are you doing here?' Before the girl could start an answer, Tindale turned back to Carter and said, 'How about some of that poison of yours, Hank?'

'Sure, Dan, sure.'

Carter didn't seem to know what to do with the shotgun, he laid it on the bar, then thinking better of that, snatched it up again and scuttled round the counter to pour whiskey one-handed.

Tindale threw back the drink, swiped his hand across his mouth, picked up the bottle and strode towards the tables. The mute scrambled out of his chair and Tindale fell into it, throwing his feet up on the table.

'And who's this?' Tindale indicated the kid.

'His name is Billy,' the girl said. 'He's my boy.'

'Say . . . you're a mama. You're a dark one, Milly. How come you never told me you had a kid. When was the last time we met? Four years ago?'

'Three and a half.'

'You never let on you had a kid then?'

'Oh, I'd left him with a cousin, and I guess I wanted to forget I was a mother for a while. Being a mother made me feel so old. Female foolishness, you'd probably call it.'

'What age is he?'

Before Milly could answer, Tindale

jumped up and strode over to Waco. He pulled back his bloodstained shirt and fingered a bandage that bound his torso.

'How you feeling, kid? It hurt?'

'It ain't so bad now, Dan.' Waco managed a smile, though his round country boy's face was ashen.

'What happened to him, Dan?' Stone asked. 'He get shot breaking out of town?'

'You doctored gunshot wounds before, haven't you?' Tindale said to Carter. 'Gonna need you to fish for a bullet in Waco. Let him have a few drinks first, though — so's he gets numb.'

Tindale sat back down again and, tossing off his whiskey, began tapping the empty glass against his chin. He glanced at the boy. 'So, this is your li'l boy, Milly? C'mere, son, lemme look at you.'

The kid looked reluctant, but he stepped forward — Tindale was the sort of person you naturally obeyed.

'What's your name, son?'

'Billy.'

'Guess you like to play around in the dirt some, huh?'

The boy stared dumbly at him.

'That shirt of yours seen better days.'

Tindale nodded, said in a low voice, 'That's OK, son,' and the boy went back over to stand beside his mother. 'Don't you believe in feeding kids, girl? He's carrying an acre of dirt on him too.'

The girl wrung her hands.

'I've just seen him myself for the first time in a year. I had to leave him here while I went to Abilene. Hank's been looking after him ever since.'

Tindale stared coldly at Carter. 'That so, huh?'

'I did my best for that there boy,' Carter protested. 'She just left him here without so much as a by-your-leave. What do I know about lookin' after young 'uns?'

'You must have let him run wild,' the girl said.

'You're a fine one — '

'All right, cut it out.' Tindale splashed more whiskey in his glass.

'Dan, what about these two jokers?' Stone jerked a thumb at Mike and Billy.

'What about them?'

'Well, what're we gonna do about them? Guess we better let 'em have a bullet apiece.'

'That ain't the way I operate.'

'They'd have killed us given half the chance.'

'That's their job. I got nothing against lawmen. Most of them's crooked, but at least they risk their lives like us. It's the so-called respectable people who pay their wages that I can't stand.' Tindale looked at the rangers. 'If we let you live, would you come after us?'

'No, I guess not,' Mike said.

'You can't trust their word, dammit,' Stone said.

'Texas Rangers?' Carter said. 'Back-shooters one and all. The only time they'll kill from the front is when they fire some Mexican village and wait to pick off the women and kids as they come runnin' out.'

'Why don't you shut your mug, melon-head,' Billy said.

Carter looked twice at Billy. He seemed uncertain whether it was Billy's choice of words or the fact that he could speak at all he objected to most, but he showed the rest of his top front teeth and some gum too as he snarled, 'Why don't I just shut yours?' and stepping forward made to drive the butt of the shotgun into Billy's head.

Billy obligingly reached out and gave Carter a hand. He caught the shotgun butt and hauled, and Carter found himself sailing past Billy, sending tables and chairs flying as he landed sprawling against the wall. Billy resettled his hat and seemed to dismiss Carter from his mind. But Carter hadn't forgotten Billy. He came back madder than ever, attacking from behind with the shotgun held by both ends, and slinging the barrel over Billy's head, stuck his knee against the back of Billy's chair and settled in to choke the life out of him.

Billy grabbed the gun by butt and barrels and heaved. Carter just grinned. Billy didn't stand a chance in this position. Carter could bring his arms and back and even his right leg to bear — Billy would have to make do with his arms and shoulders.

Still, he was finding it would take a little bit of work at least. Carter screwed his eyes tight shut and made a slot of his mouth to show his gritted teeth. The colour of his face began to deepen to a brick red.

Billy's shoulders bulged. His shirt strained at its yoke and socket seams, strained at the buttons till his chest hair showed between. For half a minute they were still as a tableau in stone — but all in the room felt the vibration of their effort as a thrill in the soles of the feet.

Then the gun began to move. There was a space between the barrel and Billy's neck. Slow as the ball of the sun clearing the eastern mountains, Billy's arms began to straighten. Billy stood. Now Carter's pumpkin head pressed against Billy's neck and his rank breath gasped into his ear. Billy's long arms straightened even more . . . straightened to the point where if Carter wanted to keep hold of the gun he would have to let his stubby arms pop their sockets.

With a final heave, Billy wrenched the shotgun free, but as he found he was looking at three pistols trained on him, he slung it on the ground. Billy stepped back, treading heavily on Carter's toes as he did. Carter hopped and Billy said:

'Sorry.'

Then: 'No, I ain't . . . '

Billy smashed the elbow end of his forearm into Carter's mouth. Carter's big head thudded on the bar counter before he hit the floor, and a few seconds later when his muzzy brain cleared he lurched for the shotgun.

'Leave it,' Tindale ordered.

'That dirty stinkin' . . . ' Blood foamed from Carter's mouth. 'He done busted a tooth on me.'

'He sure as hell has,' Tindale agreed. 'You look like a piano that's threw a key.'

Billy winked at the kid and saw him smile for the first time yet.

'Why don't you clean yourself up,' Tindale told Carter, 'then you can have a look at Waco. Me, I'm gonna go feed the fleas.'

'Wait, Dan,' Stone said. 'What are we gonna do about these two? You know we can't let them live.'

'Quit bleatin' at me, Stone,' Tindale said. 'I'm beat and I'm saddle-numb and it's either lie down or drop. So, goodnight one and all.'

Tindale walked to the side door, and as he opened it he looked back. Milly's eyes locked with his and her face took on a glow. Tindale stepped through the door and left it open a crack behind him.

Milly got up and followed Tindale through the door.

11

Mercifully for Waco, he lost consciousness soon after Carter started on him with a kitchen knife. Blood slopped on the tables that Waco lay across, while Carter, fuddled with rotgut, rummaged with the knife. At a time like this, he regretted his lies about being an army surgeon; though in the war the identity of the dead doctor he'd stolen had kept him out of the fighting — for a while at least. The carnage he created amongst the wounded didn't go unnoticed long even in the confusion of battle, and if he hadn't deserted they doubtless would have strung him up.

Carter's greasy face dripped sweat into the raw meat of Waco's side as he poked and sliced and squelched around, trying to trace the track of the lead. Like an old hound whose nose has gone, Carter was lost, and not knowing which way to turn, tried first one way then the other. The dirty point of the kitchen knife sliced and prodded and Waco's guts oozed like pricked sausages, until finally the knife nicked Waco's aorta. Startled by the spray of blood, Carter snatched back the knife, slicing as he did so all-but-through the artery.

'Goddam, it's rainin' blood,' Stone said as he dodged clear of the arterial jet.

Mike stepped across and, ripping away the sleeve of Waco's shirt at the seam, balled it up and stuffed it into his side. The others drew close again now the blood had ceased to sprinkle. Billy bent over Waco's ashen face and peeled back an eyelid.

'Melon-head done hit the jackpot that time. Ain't enough in his veins to keep his eyes bloodshot.'

'That slug got to come out,' Carter said. 'Otherwise he'll die of lead poisonin'. I seen it in the war a hunerd times.'

'Lead poisoning's the least of his worries,' Mike said. 'The way you were working on him, looked like you were dicing meat for a stew.'

Mike lifted away the sopping cotton plug.

'Least the blood's stopped,' Carter said.

'It stopped because his heart stopped pumping,' Mike said. 'He's dead.'

'You two get back over there,' Stone said, then looking round: 'Where's the kid?'

'That little runt creeps about like a rat beneath the floorboards. Could be anywhere. Don't worry about him.' Carter wiped his bloody hands on his vest. 'I'm more worried about these two. My operation here will be finished if Dan lets these hound-dogs go.'

'We ain't letting nobody go,' Stone said.

'Yeah, Dan'll see sense when he gets a night's sleep.'

'Don't worry about Dan. He'll have forgot all about these'uns. When he wakes up and sees they're gone, he won't even mention it.'

The mute began to gesture and grunt.

'Abe reckons he wants to do it,' Stone said. 'Abe's just like an old tomcat when it comes to killin' — takes a pleasure in it.'

'I gotta notion to see off Toothless Joe here,' Carter said. 'It's up to you.'

'Hell, Abe can do it. I feel weak as a kitten. Can't take no more botheration of the nerves tonight.'

Stone nodded. 'OK, Abe. Take the big one outside and shoot him good. Make sure with a brain shot.'

The mute motioned with his pistol.

'Been nice knowin' you, Cap'n,' Billy said. 'Kinda yearn to have cracked this here butterball's fat gourd open, but otherwise it been a good life and I got no regrets.'

'Meet you in the happy hunting ground, Billy.'

'Sure, Cap'n. I be seein' you.'

Carter sniggered. 'Hee, hee, hee

— happy huntin' ground — y'hear, Stone? Happy hogwash. But you'll meet up soon enough, don't worry. Gonna be a couple of sorry ghosts, moanin' and a groanin' as they goes hauntin' the sagebrush, just a'scoopin' itty bits of ghost brain like lumpy oatmeal and tryin' to smear it back in the holes in their damn heads. Haw, haw, haw.'

Billy took a step towards Carter, and Carter scuttled back to the bar to snatch up his shotgun.

'Come on, gap-teeth. Come on, mule-ears.' Carter jammed the shotgun butt into his shoulder. 'I might just change my mind and take you outside myself.'

Billy curled his lip.

'I don't reckon you got the guts to even backshoot.'

Billy turned to the mute. 'Come on, you gruntin' hog, what you waitin' for?' he said, and headed for the door.

'Wait,' Stone said. 'I'm glad he tried that on you, Carter. Might have tried similar on Abe. Never know with a desperate man. Just to make extra sure . . . ' Stone slipped Waco's bandanna from round his neck, and going up behind Billy bound his hands with it. Then they shoved Billy at the door.

The mute grunted and prodded with his pistol and directed Billy round behind the side of the stable. He pushed Billy against the boards of the stable, rammed the gun into his neck, forcing his cheek flat against the boards.

The barrel drew back from his neck, and Billy listened to a cricket click its legs somewhere in the sage and heard through the boards the hoot of an owl up in the stable beams and the answering wicker of the horses. The seconds drew out very slowly, while Billy worked at coming to terms with the fact of his ceasing to be. A part of him stood back and watched his brain doing its darndest, squeezed for time as it was, to make the best of things, just the way it had reconciled him to a hundred other misfortunes in his life, from losing his front teeth, to getting jilted by some girl, to being passed over for promotion, and way back to the time when a beloved colt had sickened and died and left him broken-hearted. Living was just a whole mess of sorrow. And when he thought of all the lives that had existed since old mother Eve dropped her first litter, and he seemed to see them all, fussing and scurrying like so many ants on a heaving hill, then . . . well, it didn't seem so much of a tragedy that Billy Barnes' little life should get squished out. Dying just seemed . . . weird . . . awful weird . . . as if all the times as a child when he'd woken up with the horrors that come in the depths of the night, this was just exactly what had been hovering above his bed in the darkness.

At the touch of the hard gun barrel in the back of his head, all those thoughts flew away like so many dreams startled by reality. The ratchet click of the hammer cocking sounded like the grinding of rock as the world split open like an almighty chestnut.

There was a bang, and Billy's soul went winging into darkness then came rushing back on the instant when it realized he wasn't dead.

The mute bellowed laughter against the back of his neck and gave another loud slap to the board by Billy's ear, and despite himself Billy jumped again.

Billy turned and looked at the mute's laughing face, saw the cruel, brainless glee in his demented eyes. Then for an instant his eyes flicked to the side at the sign of a movement in the weeds, but instantly he locked his stare on the mute's again.

The kid rose out of the weeds, his mouth twisted and his eyes wide and dazed with horror, and the moonlight flashed for an instant on the blade of Billy's knife. The mute's laughter soared to a howl and he clutched his haunch at the same moment that Billy cannoned into him and sent him sprawling. Billy trampled through the weeds and brought his boot heel down on the mute's forehead and as he lay dazed, Billy dropped on his chest and hissed, 'Cut me, Billy. Cut me free.' He couldn't see the kid, but he felt the neck cloth strain at his wrists and his hands flew apart just as the mute came round. They rolled together in the weeds and Billy grabbed the mute's gun hand and clamped his free hand over his mouth. The mute bucked and squirmed beneath him but, fuddled from the kick, all his effort was as undirected as the whipping of a snake with a squashed head. Billy forced the gun round towards the mute's face and snatching his hand away from his mouth squeezed the mute's own finger on the trigger. The mute's howl for help was drowned in the blast of the gun. Powder stung Billy's eyes as blood splashed his face, and for a moment he could see nothing for the swirling smoke that made him hack and retch as he gasped it into his lungs.

When he could see through the smoke, he made out enough to know that the mute would give him no more trouble. He got up and turned, gun in hand, to face the kid. The kid gazed in horror at Billy's gore-splattered face.

'You did good,' Billy gasped. 'You did good, Little Billy.'

Billy laid a hand on the boy's bony shoulder. He was trembling, his knees knocking together, his teeth chattering with fright.

'You just take it easy, son.'

'I never stabbed nobody before,' the kid said in a voice that had developed an opera singer's vibrato. 'With a knife.'

'You're pretty good at it. A pretty fair stabber. Done saved my hide for me. You're about the first kid I knew that ever done that, to my recollection. But I suspected the first time I seed you you'd be a good man in a tight spot — b'lieve I remarked as much to my partner Mike. I knowed you wouldn't let ol' Ranger Billy down when it came to the crunch.'

'I sure wouldn't. Not if it come to the crunch.'

118

'But you done enough work for one night, considerin' you ain't even growed up yet. So I want you to take it easy for a spell, catch your breath back. You know any good little nooks or hidey-holes you could squirrel into till I holler for you to come out?'

'Yeah, I know a mess of 'em. I know one in the stable too.'

'Is it good?'

'I reckon it's so good that nobody would har'ly ever find me there.'

'Well, now, why don't you go and slip in there, and just rest up for a spell?'

'OK.'

The boy turned and slipped away and Billy followed his passage by the shimmering of the weeds in the moonlight. Then Billy checked the mute's gun and headed for the house.

12

The crack of a pistol shot broke the night's stillness, and Carter clutched his guts and staggered. He lurched towards Mike and croaked:

'I'm done for, Cap'n. Guess this is the end of the trail for your ol' pal Toothless Billy. But don't you fret, Cap'n dear, and don't you shed no tear for your dear dead frien'. 'Cause we'll meet up by and by. Up yonder there beyond the blue, blue sky. And with a hearty shake o' the hand I'll cry, 'Welcome, Cap'n, dear, to the happy huntin' ground'. Haw, haw, haw.'

'Your turn next, ranger,' Stone said. 'Time to take that last walk. How you feel about that?'

'That's OK, Stone,' Mike said.

What he felt was alone. And though these two were jabbering in his ear, they might have been a couple of ghosts. Just as much ghosts as the dead man on the table, or Billy, who had gone and left him alone, let him down, like everything lets you down. Because there was nothing you could depend upon. The boards he stood on seemed as insubstantial as an old memory, and it was hard to believe they had seemed so real.

'That's OK, is it?' Stone echoed. 'Couple a minutes' time you'll be lyin' out there spewin' up your blood.'

'Don't worry, Stone, the rangers will track you down,' Mike said, though he felt he was just reciting lines like some preacher who'd lost the call and didn't give a damn any more. 'Track you down and string you up. My regret is I won't be there to watch you do that old Tennessee waltz myself.'

'Talkin' about dancin' . . . I bet you dance real sweet. That there Swede could dance now. 'Bout danced his hind legs off, that Swede — once he got warmed to it. Still, he wasn't young — was shufflin' kind of near the grave's edge. Not like you — straight and high and in your prime. I bet you could dance that there Swede into a cocked hat if you tried. I bet you's a real pretty dancer. How about steppin' us a little jig before you go? No? Oh, yes, I promise you you'll dance if I set my mind to it.' At the creak of the batwing doors, Stone said, 'Abe, 'member how that Swede danced — '

'Ol' Abe's nothin' but a memory hisself, butterball.'

Mike felt the chill of death dispelled. Billy's vitality filled the room, seemed to set the very molecules of the air vibrating.

Stone, white-cheeked, rose slowly from the chair with his eyes riveted on Billy's gory face.

Billy nodded at the shotgun that Carter held with the barrels dipped floor-wards.

'Only two ways that scattergun got of goin' — either bring it up or drop it down.'

'The ranger's a sport, Hank — stepping through the door with his gun in his belt.' Stone tried for a mocking tone, but the tight muscles of his windpipe forced a high edge on it.

'Sure,' Billy said. 'I was curious to know what you boys was made of. I know what you're made of, melon-head — lard 'n' hog-rind.'

As Billy talked, Stone was edging to the wall, opening the gap between him and Carter, so that Billy would have a wider area to cover.

Mike stepped over to the side door, in case Tindale decided to join the party.

'What's it gonna be, melon-head?' Billy said. 'That ol' thunder-tube only got to swing up a couple inches. Could sure give me a belly ache from where you're standin'.' Billy let his eyes swivel over to Stone. 'You was aimin' to make my partner dance, huh? Guess you'd of thunk twice if you'd ever seen him — 'bout the most awkward cuss that ever stomped a lady's corns. Hear you made Farmer Carl dance too — kind of pertic'ler for dancin', ain't you? How'd

123

you like to see me dance? For two cents, I'd dance on your face, butter-ball.'

'OK, Carter,' Stone said. 'You can bring that gun up before he can get anywhere near his. Just do it.'

The shotgun trembled in Carter's hand.

'Come on,' Stone said, 'just do it.'

Fear mixed with recklessness gave Stone's eyes a mad look. The stink of his adrenalin hung in the air.

'All right, just do it.'

The words, squeezed out of the side of his mouth in a tight whisper, were to nerve himself as much as Carter.

'Just do it . . . NOW — '

Stone was fast. He slid the Colt all the way out of its holster before the shot from Billy's .45 punched through his breastbone and sent a gout of thick heart's blood leaping past his closing eyes. In swirling gun smoke, Billy's pistol swung as he thumbed the hammer back.

The shotgun and Stone's body hit

the floor at the same time and the row of glasses on the shelf rattled, while a bottle on the counter keeled right over and spewed an ounce of rotgut from its neck.

Carter raised his hands but couldn't keep them still. They pawed and plucked at his filthy vest. His eyes, bleared with whiskey rheum, bulged at the .45's one black eye staring back at him.

'Don't shoot.'

'Why not?' Billy enquired.

'Because I give up.'

'You can give up till it brings on a nosebleed, far as I give a damn.'

'You caint shoot an unarmed man. You're a lawman.'

'That's right. A ranger. We generally tends to shoot unarmed Mexican women and kids, but I guess we could make an exception for an unarmed feller like you. In fact this ain't ranger work, this is personal. You're a fun-lovin' little feller, ain't you? Must've had some high old times whuppin' little kids with the old hickory stick and half starvin' them to death 'n such. You won't feel half so cheerful when I get done. Never fails — a chunk of hot lead a'gnawin' and a'gripin' at the guts, and a feller'll feel that ol' enthusiasm just leak away, liable to turn downright hangdog.'

Carter began to move in a curious fashion. It was as if he was trying to shrink by drawing his head into his shoulders and his chest into his belly — his arms even seemed to draw further into their sockets. He crossed his legs and bent over, as if to protect his privates, and his hands moved from here to there, though each time they covered one part of his body he took fright at baring another, so his hands never did keep still. Turning to the side, he added a forward heading to all these other antics, and the result was a strange dance that carried him round the bar counter and out of sight.

'Get out of there, Carter,' Billy said.

Carter's voice came in a sulky

tremolo from behind the counter.

'I ain't.'

'Don't make me come and get you.'

'I ain't comin' out, 'cause you're only gonna shoot me.'

'That's right.'

'Oh, Jesus . . . why does this have to happen to me? I never asked that damned whore to leave that kid here. He was just dumped on ol' muggins Hank to look after. But I never drove him off. I fed him. And not content with all the trouble he's give me, now that damned sneakin' little runt is gonna get me killed over the head of him. Well, I've learned my lesson, I swear. Next kid that anybody just lights out and dumps on me can root, hog or die for all I care. It weren't askin' much just to be left in peace in this mis'able shack with nothin' but the damned sagebrush all around. I'd just like to know who laid down the law that says Hank Carter ain't ever supposed to have one solitary ounce of luck. I just hope you can live with yourself after you put a bullet in me. 'Cause there must be a Lord up there watching ev'thing and a'reckonin' up, and he knows I had my share of trouble and it just ain't right to kill me, so it ain't.'

'See what you done, Billy?' Mike said.

From behind the counter came the sound of wailing.

'He's started crying too.'

'Aw, Cap'n, how was I to know he was gonna take on so? Back in the old days I seen outlaws laugh off a bullet in the guts and say it didn't hardly hurt at all. Johnny Preston, that rode with his brothers Sam and Joey, I put a hole you could fit your fist in right through his belly, and he just looked at me kind of disgusted and said, 'Is that the best you can do?' Why, I 'member — '

'We ain't done yet,' Mike said picking up the shotgun. 'Let's get Tindale?' He nodded in the direction of the counter. 'Bring him along.'

Billy went behind the bar and grabbed a fistful of shirt collar.

Thinking his last moments had come, Carter began to yelp like a pup.

'If you don't shut up I *will* kill you,' Billy hissed.

Carter's yelping changed to a stifled moaning. Billy manhandled him through the side door. There were four doors leading off the narrow corridor beyond.

'Open it,' Mike ordered Carter and Billy shoved him at the first door.

Carter turned the handle and pushed the door, then scuttled out of the way.

The moonlight coming through the window was almost as bright as lamplight. An unmistakable reek of Carter hung above the mess, otherwise the room was empty. In the second room, the girl sat white-faced on the edge of the bed beside the open window. There was no sign of Tindale.

Carter wasn't quick enough to clear out of the way and got a shoulder in the face as Billy turned and ran back out, closely followed by Mike. They burst out through the batwings in time to see

Tindale ride out of the stable. Billy threw up his pistol and fired. Horse and rider went down, but the figure of the man detached itself from the horse and a flash of orange flame spurted from it. As they scattered to each side of the door that framed them as targets, the bullet buzzed above their heads and hit the boards of the shack with a 'thock'. The horse lay on the ground, whickering and feebly trying to raise its head, but there was no sight of Tindale.

'Come on,' Mike said and began running over to the side of the stable.

Billy followed and sprinted through the weeds all the way round the stable to come at the door from the other side. As they edged towards the door there was a blast and the door lit for an instant, then came a confusion of neighing and pounding hoofs and a stampede of horses through the open doorway. They came out in a tight cluster so that all that was visible in the moonlight was a dark mass of surging heads and flying manes and neither

Mike nor Billy spotted Tindale stretched the length of an animal's back until it was too late to get a good shot, and soon all they could see of the fleeing horses was a cloud of dust above the sage.

Billy went over to the wounded horse and shot a bullet into its brain. Opening the saddle-bag that wasn't pinned under its body he said:

'At least he didn't get his loot.'

'What's that?' Mike pointed to a shape coming towards them through the sage from the direction in which Tindale and the horses had run.

As the horse trotted closer, Billy said:

'That there nag of mine is what you call my evil demon. It gives me a sly look sometimes that's right peculiar. Don't know what exactly its got on its mind, but I reckon it has business to settle with me one of these days.'

13

They dug graves for the dead outlaws next day and buried them with a semblance of Christian decency. When they'd finished Mike said to Billy:

'We're in a fix with one horse between us.'

'The old farmer's place is two days' ride from here. Why don't one of us ride over there, pick up some mounts and ride back?'

'We don't know if he had any more than one mount. I guess that's better than nothing, but what if Stone and Caffrey set fire to the place after they got done killing old Carl? One of us might ride two days to find the farmer's horse just a smouldering heap in a burnt-out stable, or gone to hell away.'

'Well, what else can we do?'

Mike called Carter over.

'Where's the nearest place to here?'

Carter scratched his armpit and looked sorry for himself. Finally he said in the hard-done-by tone he used with the rangers now:

'There's a mining camp twenty miles to the east.'

Billy brightened up at this news. 'Twenty miles ain't so bad,' he said to Mike.

'No, I guess we could do twenty miles,' Mike agreed.

'It's abandoned now though.'

Billy's face fell again. 'Carter, I'm gonna slap your head.'

'I guess that's all you're good for,' Carter muttered.

'What?' Billy demanded.

'So where is the nearest place?' Mike said.

'The Wilberforce place is a day's ride beyond the old mining camp.'

'Do the Wilberforces still live there?' Billy said. 'I'd like to 'stablish that.'

'Yeah, there's a man and wife and a couple-three young'uns. Got a couple of hired men too, they run some cattle.'

'Good,' Mike said. 'That's where we'll head.'

They loaded up with food and water, then mounted the girl and the boy on Billy's horse and started off.

Riding in front of his mother with her arms around him, the kid looked as happy as Billy had ever seen him. The girl was sad and silent and for a long while the boy was too shy to speak to her, but finally he said:

'Am I gonna live with you now?'

'I don't know,' the girl said.

The glow began to seep out of the boy's face.

'Well, I'd sure like to,' he said with a forlorn note.

'I might have to go away, Billy,' the girl said, and glanced towards the rangers.

'When?'

'When we get to where the rangers are taking us.'

'But I'd come with you, if you wanted.'

'You wouldn't be able to come with me, I'm afraid.'

'But where do you have to go to?'

'It's a place where bad people go.'

'I never knew you was bad.'

'Hush, Billy.'

'I never knew you was bad, so why you gotta go to that place?'

'Ask the rangers.'

The boy turned to Billy and said, 'I was fixin' to go live with my mama.'

Billy glared at the track ahead of him and didn't answer.

'I can't har'ly believe she's bad, 'cause it's the first I heard of it.'

The boy's anxiety grew as he gazed at Billy, who strode on, looking neither to right or left and frowning fiercely. He reached down and twitched the sleeve of Billy's shirt.

'Mister . . . my mama says when — '

'Hell fire . . . ' Billy turned and glared at Mike as he said, 'Tell your mama to cross her bridges when they come. There's a mess of things can happen between now and then.'

'Take it easy, Billy,' Mike said.

'Hell, you take it easy. What's that kid

gonna do without his mama?'

'She stole a diamond necklace.'

'She never did,' the boy cried. 'My mama never did steal nothin'.'

'That's right, kid,' Billy said, still glaring fiercely at Mike. 'She never stole no necklace, she just borrowed one for a spell, and now she's 'bout ready send it back again.'

'Goddam,' Mike said, 'can't you even stop jawin' for ten minutes?' They travelled on in silence but for the clop of the horse's hoofs and the scuffling of their feet in the dust, then Mike burst out: 'That damn female ain't been with us a day and already we're arguing.'

The boy looked distressed at Mike's outburst, but for some reason the girl brightened up. She began to hum and the boy was happy to see his mother happy. The boy would need new clothes, the girl said. She said she would buy him a suit of clothes that she'd seen a little French boy in New Orleans wearing, with a floppy bow tie and a little gold velvet waistcoat and shoes with silver buckles. Early spring sunshine shone on the sage, and as they walked along Billy tried to keep the boy cheered by naming the birds that flew out of the breaks, and once he spotted an eagle riding the thermals and pointed it out to the boy who craned up at the little speck high up in the deep blue distance overhead. The girl smiled at Billy with gratitude.

When they stopped to camp, the girl sat beside Billy. The boy was happy to see them talking together. He was proud of his mother and proud of his friend Billy. Now and then he would butt into the conversation with a subject of his own, talking about the toads he'd seen by the stagnant pool in Alfalfa Flats, or speculating on how high a man could jump.

After a while the smile left the girl's face and she sat and gazed wistfully at her small neat hands folded in her lap. Billy watched the girl's mood affect the boy. He saw how he tried to cheer her. When chattering didn't help, he tried pretending to trip and fall on the ground. Then he squatted down and rolled head-over-heels in the dust. His tumbles became more frantic, and the happy face he forced struggled to hide another expression, desperate and help-less, that Billy caught glimpses of, glistening in his eyes, as he glanced at her for her reaction. He remembered a horse he had seen struggling in deep mud. A sense of desperation had dawned then among the watchers with the realization that soon, no matter how it struggled, it would be beyond help. They could put a rope round its neck — but they could pull its head off before they would free it from the mud. The animal had known it too. And its struggles became more frantic as its panic grew. Billy's hands twitched. He wanted to reach out and lend the boy the strength of his big hands. He could almost taste the despair the boy struggled in, waiting to fill his mouth and gullet like mud, till he choked on the thick, cold taste of it.

'Goddam . . . that boy . . . ' Billy trailed off and glared down at his big hands.

The girl looked up, her eyes dim and guilty.

'Billy,' she called. 'Come and give mama a hug.'

The boy ran over and threw his arms around her and rested his face on her breast. The girl's eyes gazed sadly at the boy's tousled head on her breast, and Billy admired how small and white her hand was as it smoothed his hair. The setting sun made a golden halo of her own light-brown hair, and stray wisps of it shimmered and danced before her eyes.

'Mama, I wish you didn't have to go,' the boy muttered against her breast.

'Billy, you go and see if you can find some more twigs for the fire,' the girl said.

When the boy had gone, she said, 'I don't mind so much for myself. I know I did wrong and I've got it coming. I just hate to leave Billy alone.'

'That didn't stop you before.'

The girl hung her head.

'It's not easy for a girl alone, but I'm not making any excuses . . . '

'What about his father?'

'All the men I've known have been kind of wild. His father's wild too. I can't depend on him. It's just me and Billy . . . and I won't be any good to him where I'm going. I've let Billy down, and I'd do anything to put it right, but there's nothing can be done.'

'Don't say that.'

'What can I do?'

'Well . . . you've made a start by feelin' remorse.'

'If it was just a question of remorse, I wouldn't have a worry in the world. When I think of the dirty, greasy men I . . . I guess I never will be clean again.'

'That's hogwash. Anybody can make their mistakes. I done my share of sinnin'. What's a sin for a woman is just as much a sin for a man, so if you're a sinner, you got good company with me.'

'You're a good man.'

'There's some would give you an argument on that.'

'No, you're good . . . decent. If only I'd met a good man when I was young, instead of the dirty, crooked, hateful animals . . . pigs wallowing in their own filth. If I'd just met somebody strong and decent . . . But it's too late now. We're all made of the same clay, but just like pots on the wheel some take a crooked shape. I guess there's only one place for a spoiled job . . . throw it on the heap.'

'So long as the clay ain't hardened you can start again.'

'If only you could.'

'If you didn't have to go to prison, what would you do?'

'I don't know. It's no good thinking about things like that.'

'Would you try and find Billy's father?'

'He wouldn't want to know about it.'

'You'd have to get some kind of work, so you could support him.'

'There's only one kind of work I know.'

'You'd have to think of something, for Billy's sake.'

'What can I do?'

'You'd have to find yourself a man, that's all. Someone who could look after you and raise Billy.'

'There's only one kind of man who's interested in the likes of me.'

'Well, I don't know. You're awful pretty. Sometimes a man dreams of a pretty girl. He gets to thinkin' that with a pretty girl to make his own, all kinds of things would begin to make sense. I think there's plenty who'd take an interest in you.'

'Like who, for instance.'

'Like me . . . oh, I'm not the kind of guy a girl dreams about. I'm the sort of guy that'll do to keep a pretty girl's plain friend company so she can walk with the guy she's interested in. But I make fifty dollars a month ranger's pay, and if I didn't run around raisin' hell I could save half of that. But a guy like me ain't got no right to ask a pretty girl.'

'What do you mean 'a guy like you'.'
'I'm ugly.'

'Oh, well, a girl can get awful sick of all these fancy blades when she finds out they're just as cheap and worthless as tin underneath the glitter.'

'Then would you consider a guy like me?'

'You're probably the best man that I've ever met, but it's just no good talking about it. The only thing certain in my future is a prison cell.'

The boy came running back dangling a lizard by the tail.

'Look 'at I got,' he said, thrusting it under Billy's nose.

'That's real nice. Why don't you show it to your mama?'

Billy got to his feet and walked over to where Mike sat cooking beans.

'How long have I been a lawman now, and I never put a foot wrong? I ain't never took no bribes, and there's plenty has.'

'Good for you,' Mike said.

The girl squealed as the boy dangled

the lizard in her eyes.

'Why don't we just send that necklace back and say we found it among Carter's stuff waitin' to be fenced.'

'We can't pin it on Carter. He never took it.'

'Well, we send it back, sayin' . . . hell, not sayin' nothin'. We just send it back and let the girl go.'

'We're lawmen.'

'So?'

'So we act according to the law. The badge we wear gives us certain powers, but once we start deciding for ourselves what's right and wrong, we're abusing those powers.'

'I guess that sort of talk goes down pretty slick in certain place, but it's wasted on me — I can't throw any weight to get you promoted.'

'What's to stop you deciding you've got the right to put a bullet in Carter's head because he deserves it?'

Carter glanced over uneasily at the mention of his name.

'I can see you runnin' for office one of these days, you're a pretty ambitious feller — and steady too.'

'There's either right or there's wrong. No inbetween.'

'Rules . . . some just love 'em. Rules makes life a whole lot less complicated for some fellers. I guess you'd hang me from a damned tree, if you had to, wouldn't you? Well once the rules get so damn sacred that a man stops listening to his own heart . . . well, then . . . to my mind he ain't even a man any more.'

'She left the kid once, who's to say she won't leave him again? Anyway, the kid's better off even in the orphanage than mixed up in her sort of life. She ain't a fit mother.'

'I reckon if you say another word I'm gonna bust your head open.'

'She's sure gotten to you somehow.'

'Yeah, she's gotten to me, and the kid has too. They both had bad luck and they need a break, and I aim to give it to them.'

'How you fixin' to do that — even if she didn't go to jail, what's she gonna do?'

'I'm gonna marry her.'

Mike looked up quick.

'You're what? Marry her? She's a whore.'

Billy grabbed Mike's shirt.

'Remember I once said I could only beat you if I thought I was in the right? Well, now I'm about ready to knock your damned head off.'

'Take it easy.'

'Like hell.'

'Billy — '

Mike pulled the necklace out of his pocket and threw it in the dust in front of Billy.

'Do what you want with it.'

Billy snatched up the necklace.

'I'll deliver it back. Say I found it or somethin'.'

'I don't even want to know.'

'God bless you, Mike.'

'Leave me alone now, Billy.'

'Sure.'

14

It began to rain in the night, and the sky was low and dark in the morning. None of them had slept much, and they were tired, wet and cold when they started off after a breakfast of coffee and hardtack biscuits.

Billy poured out an endless stream of chatter, and when he raised a laugh from the boy or a smile from the girl he turned he looked up at them on the horse grateful as a faithful hound that's finally been taken notice of.

The rest of them were mostly silent though, and at one point Carter turned his big sullen face to Mike and muttered, 'Don't he ever shut up?'

Mike ignored Carter, tried to ignore Billy's chatter, as he tried to ignore the wind that pasted his wet shirt to his chest and the drizzle sifting from the huge grey waste overhead.

A clump of shacks huddled on the horizon, grew bigger and ever more dismal as they approached, until they crowded them round like crippled beggars, crooked doors gaping like toothless mouths, the torn tarpaper roofs and the greased paper of the windows hanging like stiff old rags. They squatted in one of the dank and filthy huts to escape the drizzle and brew coffee to warm them.

'A prospector called McGee seeded this place with gold,' Carter said. 'Then he sold off claims at a hundred dollars apiece, till a whole bunch of gold-hungry fools crowded in here, dreamin' they'd be rich like Crackus. One sorry joker who'd sold ever'thing he had in the world to make one last stab at it ended up shootin' wifey and itty-bitty baby before turnin' that ol' scattergun on hisself.'

This was the sort of joke that appealed to Carter and he laughed good and hard.

Billy sat with the girl and the kid, full

of solicitude, racking his brains for ways to lift the dreary spell of the place that weighed their spirits down.

'When we get to Pinewood, we'll fix you up first off at the boarding house where I stay. But that'll only be temp'ry, 'cause I figure I could get me a loan from the bank and buy a plot on the north side of town and some timber to start buildin' a little house. I reckon, to save money, you know, we could move in soon as I built the ground floor. But it ain't gonna be no shack at all — gonna be a proper storey house. I could build the rest as we's livin' there. Gonna have two storeys and an attic too. Though I reckon, once we get started, we could go as high as we took the notion to go. Gonna have a little fenced off garden at the front — and, hell, one at the back too. And we could have us a porch to the front to set on in the summer evenin's, and . . . '

As Billy rambled on, Carter snickered into his coffee and whispered to Mike, 'I guess while he's out rangerin' she could do a little work from home.'

Billy looked over, and Carter quit snickering and began blowing in his coffee instead. A moment later, though, he showed his big eyeteeth again and winked at Mike. 'Just to help pay the bills, you know?'

Billy stood up, and Carter quit snickering and began huffing in his coffee so the steam billowed round his ears.

'What'd you say?'

'Me? Never said nothin'.'

'What did you say about work from home?'

'I said she could work from home, that's all.'

Billy knocked the cup out of Carter's hand.

Carter hunched down and muttered sulkily, 'I don't know what's wrong with him.'

'Shut up, you,' Mike said. 'Forget it, Billy.'

'I just said work from home. Never said what sort of work.'

Billy's big hand shot out and Carter came up like a dog hoist by the scruff, his pumpkin head all but buried in his coat collar, then Billy slammed him into the wall of the hut so that the rotten timbers quaked and dirt spilled down on their heads.

Carter was grinning like a skull, strangling himself on high-pitched, convulsive laughter.

Billy showed him his knuckles an inch from his eyes, and said, 'I give you two seconds to quit laughin' then I'm gonna kill you with this here fist.'

But Carter didn't stop. Billy threw back his right leg to steady himself, then he drew back his arm and his whole upper body, and Mike barely jumped to his feet in time to grab the fist that was set to cave in Carter's face.

'Lemme go. I told him to stop laughin'. He's still laughin'.'

'He can't help it,' Mike said. Mike's two hands strained and trembled trying to hold Billy's wrist. 'Goddam it, Billy, I'm gonna lay the barrel of my gun across your skull . . . I'm warning you.'

Billy opened his fist, and with a heave of his left hand on Carter's collar slung him, still laughing, to the dirt floor.

Billy went back over to squat beside the nervous girl and boy, while Carter lay in the dirt, not laughing now, casting apprehensive glances at Billy.

Mike stood up and with a twitch of the hand emptied his half-full cup on the fire. Waiting for the others to finish, he stirred with his foot the pages of an old review that mouldered in the dirt. 'THE SENSATION OF THE SEASON' it said, and showed a rot-eaten print of an actress whose rosebud mouth would be shrivelled now in the grave. He stepped outside, impatient to be quit of the huddle of skewed shacks, oppressive with their ghosts of spoiled dreams and hopes disappointed.

Beyond the shanty, the ground turned marshy where it bottomed out to the stretch of the Sabine River that the miners had sifted for its illusory gold. They had to pick their way among clumps of water reeds and groves of monstrous weed, and at times the solid ground disappeared leaving them to drag through a black slurry that sucked at their heels, choked them with the rank gases their footsteps released.

A stave rose out of the slime with something painted on its crosspiece, but so faded that they had to squelch right up to it before they could vaguely make out the words:

HIS WAY.

They gazed at it dull-eyed, unable to shape whatever questions it stirred in them and unwilling to speak in the marsh's silent gloom, and so filed past into an opening in the wall of reeds.

Carter trudged ahead, and as Mike pushed a tangle of vegetation from his face, he saw that though Carter went through the motions of walking, he made no progress forward. His arms swung, and his hips swung, and his legs swung too at the knees, but his feet were motionless in the mud that covered his boots to the ankle.

'Quit moving,' Mike said.

But Carter did not stop, and trying to free his feet succeeded only in sinking them deeper.

'Quit moving,' Mike said. 'You're in quicksand.'

Carter fell still, but already the thick slime was up to the middle of his calf.

'Chris'sake, I'm goin' down,' Carter said, and another half-inch of boot leather disappeared as he said it.

'I said don't move, Goddam it,' Mike told him, as Carter began to struggle once more. 'You move again, we'll never get you out.'

Carter managed to restrain himself, but you could see that it went against every instinct.

Billy came up, and taking in the situation said, 'He's gonna have to leave them boots.'

Billy edged towards Carter till his own feet began to sink too far into the slime, then he reached out and grabbed Carter's arm.

'Shuck your foot out of your boot,' Billy said.

Carter, leaning on Billy's arm, heaved and squirmed till his dirty sockless foot cleared his left boot. This activity had worked his right foot into the mud to below the knee. Billy worked his head under Carter's shoulder and his arm under his left knee, while Mike, grabbing Billy round the waist, helped haul until Carter came free of his remaining boot and all three lay in a heap on half-solid ground.

'Have to find another way round this,' Mike said.

They filed back past the signpost with its weird inscription until they found another avenue in the reeds, down which they trudged, Mike in front, followed by a barefoot Carter, while bringing up the rear Billy led the horse that carried the girl and boy. But they hadn't gone far, though far enough in the sucking mud to turn their legs to lumps of lead, when up ahead appeared another stave. They

155

approached — squinting, sweat-stung eyes fixed on the ominous sign, with its skewed silhouette doubled in the reflecting mud — until they were close enough to read the message painted on the crosspiece. The letters, faded as they were, had this time worn better; they said:

THIS WAY.

And they made out too, pointing to their right, a painted arrow.

15

'Guess those miners charted the swamp,' Mike said.

They followed the direction of the sign, and after some more trekking came to another that indicated one of two paths through the reeds. A clearing opened, and ankle-deep in water they splashed across. Mike in front heard a crack, but his dull nerves did not respond, nor did his brain register alarm at a little splash among the ripples at his feet and the series of splashes darting across to the verge of reeds as if a flat pebble had skimmed the water.

Billy shouted, 'Run', but Mike was already running, sweeping the boy off the horse as Billy grabbed the girl. Carter like a prancing elephant in the lead, they reached the verge they'd started from in a welter of splashes, and hid crouching in the reeds. The horse stood motionless in the middle of the clearing, only its reflection shimmering slightly as the ripples faded and the water grew still again. Billy put two fingers to his mouth to whistle for it, but Mike grabbed his hand.

'Don't call. It'll give us away if it comes.'

'Who do you reckon let off the shot?' Billy said.

'Your guess is as good as mine.'

'It don't matter who it was,' Carter said. 'What matters is that we get out of here.'

'Keep still,' Mike said. 'It's more dangerous to move than stay. Whoever is out there knows kind of where we are now, but once we start to shake those reeds he'll know exactly.'

'What are we gonna do?' Billy said. 'We can't stay here all day.'

'You got any suggestions?' Mike said.

Billy turned to the boy. His two legs sticking out of the water were no thicker than reeds themselves as he stood blinking slowly, gazing at nothing.

'You all right, son?'

The boy didn't answer. Billy squatted down, put a hand on his shoulder and felt a faint continuous tremor. The boy showed no reaction to Billy's touch and though Billy stared directly into his eyes he couldn't seem to reach him.

'Don't fret,' Billy whispered, staring into the boy's eyes with the feeling that he might just as well be gazing at a painting for all the boy was aware of him.

A frog splashed among the reeds. The frog's round eye looking out of the side of its head gave no sign whether it saw them or gave damn if it did, and with another spring it was gone, plopping somewhere out of sight.

'Ain't nobody gonna hurt you long as ol' Billy's around,' Billy said.

The boy's head turned slowly on the spindle of neck that hardly seemed strong enough to carry its weight.

'Mama . . . '

At the word, the girl swallowed, then

had to swallow again, then her hands went to her eyes as the tears began to flow. The boy waded to her and wrapped his thin arms round her legs. Billy stood awkwardly beside her, with a hand hovering indecisively by her shoulder, as if he wanted to reassure her but couldn't quite find the courage to touch her.

'Don't cry,' he said. He looked set to cry himself the way he stood blinking helplessly with his toothless mouth ajar.

'I just want out of this place.' Her voice hitched miserably and she began crying again.

'I know,' Billy said. 'I know. We'll get you out. This godforsaken swamp . . . not even the sound of a bird to cheer you, and nothing to look at but the damned reeds just a stirrin' to and fro and the sky looking up at you from your feet. It's enough to get on anybody's nerves without somebody startin' poppin' shots at you too. We got to move, Mike.'

'Don't do nothing hasty.'

'They say one of the old miners stayed on here when all the others quit,' Carter said. 'Could've been him that shot at us, thinkin' we'd come after his gold.'

'What gold?'

'There's nothin' like gold-fever to turn a man crazy. Just think of him, camped out here all these years, keepin' on a'searchin' for his pay dirt, dreamin' of gold so long he prob'ly can't even hardly tell after a while what's wakin' and what's sleepin'. He'd be crazier than a loon by now.'

'Ain't we feelin' morbid enough, Carter?'

'What's that?'

'He's comin'.'

'It's the damned horse.'

Carter got on his knees and poked his head as close to the edge of the reeds as he dared.

'Shoo. Get out of here. Scoot, you damned swayback, a'fore you give us away.'

The horse took no notice and

continued to splash towards them. It pushed right in among them so it could nuzzle Billy's neck.

Carter sat down in the water and wrapped his arms over his head.

'He's gonna start now. Gonna start poppin' now, you'll see. That crazy prospector. Oh, Christ, I got pins and needles all over.'

Billy pulled the horse's head down so that it would not show above the reeds.

They stood motionless and quiet as the minutes crawled by. The only thing that broke the silence was a feeble little whine. Billy slapped his neck. A moment later Mike slapped his too, and soon they were all swatting and slapping at themselves.

The air danced with mosquitoes. The boy buried his head in his mother's skirts, and Carter flapped his arms around his head. The horse began to toss its mane and wicker.

'We gonna get eat alive,' Billy said.

They slapped their faces and flapped their hands about their ears. They could

162

hardly see each other for the dancing cloud of insects. The girl cried out and the boy splashed round in circles. Carter yelped and cursed. They were a heap of maddened nerve-endings. Unable to think straight, they stumbled out of the reeds, ran splashing across the clearing, and the mosquitoes followed like a dancing black cloud. The flat little crack went barely noticed in their misery and confusion. The gun cracked again and Mike's mind flipped back to the time when as a kid he'd run full-tilt into a cart rail. His right leg wouldn't hold him — it folded like a reed and he went down into the water. Billy hauled him up and they stumbled on across the clearing. The gun cracked again, and Carter yelled but kept on going, and then they were running down the avenue on the far side of the clearing. They stumbled blindly, unable to avoid roots and rocks, falling, and every time Billy went down, he thought he would never find the strength to haul Mike to his feet again, but no matter how difficult it was to move, it was impossible to stay still and remain sane under that mosquito blanket.

The insects began to thin eventually, until finally they were gone and they sat on a downed log and scratched till their faces, arms and ankles were red and their fingernails were smeared with blood. Billy's horse came trotting through the reeds. It stopped and stood with legs splayed on either side of its squat little barrel chest and fixed them all with a baleful stare.

Billy cut open Mike's pants and looked at his wound. There was a little blue-rimmed gash in the front of his thigh and a hole in the back. The hole wasn't too big, the bullet hadn't flattened or broken by the looks of it, but had carried straight on out.

'You'll live to tell the tale,' Billy said. 'You feel you could sit a horse?'

'I feel all right.'

'Sure, partner.' Billy grinned his toothless grin.

Mike smiled back, and tried to put

some of the old feeling into it. But some of the feeling had gone since Billy had turned on him over the necklace. He couldn't help it. They'd been good friends, but you couldn't help a thing like that. Anyway, he'd enough to worry about: the wound was neat, but he worried about this stinking water contaminating it. Or if one of the mosquitoes had left him a dose of fever, it wouldn't take much on top to kill him.

'What about me?' Carter said.

Billy's grin turned sour.

'What about you?'

'How am I expected to walk with this?'

Carter pointed to one of his bare feet. There was a swelling big as an apple on the ankle.

'I twisted it.'

'If you can't walk, you're gonna have to hop.'

'Then I'll just lay here and die. I guess the rangers just look out for their own and be damned to all the rest.'

'Quit belly-aching,' Mike said. 'You can ride with me.'

'I'm afraid you're gonna have to walk,' Billy said to the girl. 'I would carry you myself . . . if it was fittin' . . . ' The girl did not reply and Billy continued, 'Anyhow I can tote the boy — pick-a-back.'

The girl nodded. Her hair was plastered to her face, her dress torn and hanging at the knees, and she sat gazing at the ground with her arms crossed at her neck and her hands slowly rubbing her plump little shoulders. Her tears had streaked her cheeks and left her eyes red-rimmed, but her face was expressionless — except for one small tuck in her full lips and her desolate eyes.

Billy averted his eyes from her exposed calves, but she was too tired to notice or care.

The boy watched her with a helpless expression, keeping close but not touching her, as if afraid that instead of giving her the comfort that he longed to, he would only disturb her with his clumsiness.

'We'll get you out of here, don't worry,' Billy said.

The girl smiled and Billy, lowering his head, returned it with humility and gratitude.

'I was thinkin' we could say she was a widow,' Billy whispered to Mike. 'When we get home . . . we could say she was a widow come from the east with her boy.'

'Sure,' Mike said.

16

'Ohh . . . Clementine was a good girl.

'Clementine was a maid.

'Clementine was a sweet lamb that never once strayed.

'Clementine went a'wand'rin'

'Down to the Company Store . . .

'Came back a dollar richer and a maid no more.'

'Why don't you shut that stinkin' hole in your fat melon head?'

Billy spoke quietly and hitched his shoulders to hoist the kid's bundle of bony limbs higher on his back.

'I guess I was forgettin' there was a lady present.'

Carter began a stifled wheezing, so that Mike, riding doubled with him on the horse, shrugged and swore as Carter's sour breath fanned his neck. Carter quit grinning when Billy stopped and stood waiting for the horse to draw level.

'What's the — '

Billy hauled Carter off the horse. He came down on his back in the mud, with the saddlebags landing beside him.

Mike turned his aching head, and licked his lips to speak, but thought better of it and turned his listless eyes once more to the track ahead. He didn't care if Billy killed Carter.

'You can walk.'

'How can I walk on my foot?'

'If you can't walk, you can set.'

Billy threw the boy up behind Mike on the horse. He picked up the sack of gold that had spilled from the saddle-bags and tossed it back in with the others, then he swung the bags on the horse's rump.

'You all right?' Billy said to the girl. 'You could put your arm round my shoulder if you liked.'

'I'm awful tired,' the girl said.

'Sure you are.' Billy stooped down. 'You just swing your arm over my shoulder and it'll help to take the weight off your legs.'

Billy stooped almost double so that the girl could reach her arm around him, then waddled along supporting her.

Carter sat in the mud for a while, but when he realized they were really going to leave him he got to his feet and hobbled along trying to catch them up. His terror at being separated and at the mercy of the crazy miner made him ignore the pain in his ankle. But the ankle wasn't about to be ignored for long. Every time his right foot touched the ground it shot a bolt of pain right up him that didn't stop till it hit the inside of his skull and popped his eyes. It made him weak all over so that he twitched and shook. He couldn't bear it any more and fell in the muck. His fat, pain-wracked face grimaced up at him from his reflection in the ooze. When the pain in his ankle had subsided enough to leave room in his brain for anything else, the terror came rushing back in. The terror could no more be ignored than the pain. It went too deep, to the marrow of his bones — the terror of being alone, abandoned in unknown and hostile terrain. He thought of the miner, ancient mad eyes blazing out of a wild tangle of hair and beard, stalking along behind, or hidden among the reeds with those fixed crazed eyes staring out at him even now. Carter quivered in one place and then another as he thought of where the bullet might strike. Or perhaps he would come up close, close enough to touch, and he might close his eyes but he would have to listen to him splash about beside him, have to smell his boot leather under his nose, as he waited for the terrible blow that would stave in his skull.

Carter began to scamper along on hands and knees. He gagged on the filthy water that splashed up into his mouth, and he imagined that his own splashing covered the splash of other footsteps.

Billy waddled along, almost crippled by his jackknifed posture, but refusing to let the pain of his leaden thighs and aching back show in his face, and even attempting a smile when he turned to the girl — though keeping his mouth closed over his bare gums.

His smile faded at the sound of Carter's wails. He stopped, gently removed the girl's arm, and somehow straightened. He took hold of the horse's rein and halted it.

'Why don't you leave him?' Mike said.

'I can't stand his whinin' no more.' Billy lifted the boy from the horse and said, 'You hitch a ride with me, son.'

At last Carter, on hands and knees and whining like a cur, caught up with them. Billy struggled with his all-but-dead weight to get him on the horse.

'It ain't fair to fool a body that way,' Carter moaned.

'Friend, if you only knowed how close you come,' Billy told him.

'I'm about kilt, and I don't care if you do leave me.'

'Shut up,' Mike said. 'And keep your

stinking breath — ' A fit of coughing choked off the rest.

Billy swung the boy up on to his back. Then he stooped and caught the girl under the knees. 'Sorry, ma'am . . . but it won't be long now, you'll see.' He lifted her in his arms.

'What are you trying to prove?' Mike said, but sounding as if he didn't care much.

Billy didn't answer, just looked at him, and started to walk.

The girl laid her head against his shoulder and closed her eyes. Billy staggered now and then, but the sight of the girl's sleeping face on his shoulder and the feel of the boy's thin arms round his neck gave strength to his weary muscles. His long legs strode out, splashing through the ooze, eating up ground, so that the horse had to pick up its pace to keep with him. He hardly saw the ground in front of him. If his foot caught or he missed his step, he recovered from his stagger in a half-run, but kept on, his head thrown back, eyes all but closed, a grimace on his lips that showed his toothless gums.

Lolling, head-sore and dry mouthed in the saddle, Mike watched him, and thought he was like a horse that's taken it's head in a run that it couldn't stop if it wanted but would have to keep up till it dropped and died. And when Billy did stop, for a moment Mike thought that sure enough he was going to keel over where he stood.

But Billy had stopped at the edge of a dip. Rotting weeds floating on an evil grey scum. Two old planks made a bridge across it.

17

Billy picked up a flat slab of rock as big as a dinner plate and threw it so it landed among the rotting weeds and leaves. It hit with a dull clap. The scum sucked it in, swallowed it with a belch, and sent a waft of gas creeping past them.

'Best take the horse over first,' Billy said.

'The horse is liable to snap those rotten timbers,' Mike said.

'If they carry the horse they'll carry the rest of us.'

'They might bear the rest of us, but not the horse.'

'I'm takin' the horse over first.'

Mike rubbed his eyes. He was too tired to argue, or even think. 'All right, take the horse over first.'

Billy squatted down beside the kid.

'You reckon you could scamper over them timbers?'

'I reckon so,' the kid said.

'I reckon so too. And it's a good thing, 'cause only you can take care of the situation we got. See, this ol' horse of mine won't be pushed, but she'll be led just like a lamb. So what you got to do is take my lasso and run with it across this quicksand. When you get to the other side, then you just shake out a loop and sling a noose over this horse's neck.'

'You mean lasso it? From over there?'

'Yep. You can do it, can't you?'

'I don't know. I never throwed a real lasso before.'

'Doggone, I keep forgettin' you're a kid. But you're kinda handy, and I 'spect you could do it on your first try.'

'Maybe.'

'Oh, wait, I was forgettin' — what if them planks was to snap or you was to fall in on your way over? I guess we better have a change of plan. Better safe than sorry, is the rangers' motto.'

Billy put the noose over the boy's head and cinched it round his waist.

'Now, if you go into that, I can pull you right out again. So, go on, take a run across there.'

The boy walked across the planks, trailing Billy's rope after him. He even stopped halfway to look in, not afraid at all.

'Now, take off the rope and lay it down on the planks.'

When the boy had done this, Billy pulled the rope back to him again. He helped Mike and Carter off the horse and sat them down among the weeds on the bank. Then he looped the noose over the horse's neck and threw the free end to the boy.

'Now, easy, just lead him over easy.'

The boy pulled the rope tight and the horse began to step along the timbers.

'Don't jerk it. Let it take it's time. You're doin' fine.'

When the horse reached the middle there was a snap as the plank under its left hind-foot broke. Billy ran over the good plank, slapped the horse as hard as he could and yelled to wake the dead. The horse and Billy scrambled on to the far bank together.

'Gonna be a little trickier now,' Billy said, looking at the broken plank which lay just underneath the surface with its two ends sticking out. 'Who's comin' next. What about you, Carter?'

'I ain't comin' next.'

'Then don't,' Mike said. 'Let the girl go next, then me. Carter can go last.'

'Can you walk?'

'Yeah. I can crawl if I have to,' Mike said.

'I ain't goin' last,' Carter said. 'When yous are all over on the other side, yous won't give a damn about me. Ol' Carter, busted foot or no, can make shift as best he can, and if he can't make it over to the other side he can stay where he is and rot.'

'One more word and I'll pitch you in myself,' Mike said.

'I wouldn't do that, Ranger.'

Tindale stepped out of the vegetation on the far side of the quicksand with a gun in his hand.

'Not that Carter don't deserve it. Mistreating the kid like he did. But the thought of it kind of turns me green. He's pretty chunky, and he'd go down fast, but not fast enough. He'd have more time than he probably liked to watch that slime rising, and him threshing about there, just settling himself deeper in the harder he struggles, and hollering and yowling till he realizes it's either shut up or take a stinking mouthful of it. Then inch by inch he'd go down till he's looking straight across it at eyeball level. Then darkness. But he's still alive under there. And his lungs are screaming at him to suck, until — ugh, damn — it'd be like snuffing up a noseful of gritty oatmeal porridge. Then again . . . he has got it coming. I can't abide a bully. And any man who'll starve and beat a defenceless kid, nothing's too bad for him. So I think I'll just come over there and shove him in.'

'Jesus Christ, Dan.' Carter's eyes were popping out of a face gone grey.

His big tombstone teeth — minus the one Billy had had knocked out — glittered.

'That's right, say your prayers.'

Tindale put a foot on the plank.

'Dan, I'm beggin' you for ol' time's sake . . . I'm beggin' you on my knees.'

Carter fell forward on his hands and knees, and tried to join his hands too, but found he needed them to keep his face from hitting the ground.

'You'd have to be mighty hard-hearted to ignore a man who's humbled hisself on his hands and knees,' Carter urged, though it didn't seem to cause him much of a struggle. He appealed to the girl. 'Milly, talk to him.'

'That's all right, Milly. I wouldn't waste my time on him. How you keepin'?'

The girl's blue eyes were fixed, glittering on Tindale's, but she said nothing.

'It's a stupid question, I suppose,' Tindale said.

Carter pushed himself off his knees,

casting spiteful glances at Tindale.

'I'll have to disarm you gentlemen,' Tindale said, and motioned for Mike and Billy to throw their weapons into the quicksand. Then he went over to the horse and had a look inside the saddle-bags.

Coming back to the edge of the pool, he said to Mike, 'Sorry to bushwhack you. I prefer to look a man in the eye when I shoot him. That's my style. But when all that money's at stake, it kind of reduces your conscience a little bit. But I'm glad I didn't kill you. You'll be all right. There's a ranch about a day from here, if you follow the track. And if you can hobble there, they'll take care of you.'

'What about me?' Carter said. 'I can't hobble three feet let alone three miles. But nobody asks about me. Three miles — you might as well kill me now.'

Tindale ignored Carter — just met Billy's eyes and gave a resigned shake of the head. Then he turned back, and pushing up his Stetson with the gun barrel tip, lowered his head and looked long at the girl.

'I got to travel light, Milly. I reckon you know how it is with me — wild and free. Got some mustang blood in my veins, I guess. Yes, it's a nomadic existence, as the feller once said, but I'll revisit you again — you'll turn round one day and there I'll be, large as life, with a Tupelo rose in my hand. But for now, I'm gonna have to ride fast and singe sagebrush, so I'll bid you so long until that day.'

Tindale strode over to the horse.

'I'll have to borrow your mount, my friend,' he said to Billy. 'My own broke a leg, and I had the recourse of shooting him. Hope you don't mind.'

Billy, standing with fists hanging and staring at the ground, didn't answer.

Tindale swung himself easily into the saddle, tipped his hat and said, '*Adios, amigos.*'

The horse only shuffled its feet a little at the shake of the bit, but stayed put.

18

The horse turned its head and its big doleful eyes gazed at Billy.

'I guess he's grew attached to you,' Tindale said. 'You must treat him well.'

'It's a she,' Billy said.

'Sorry, girl, but it looks like I'm gonna have to be . . . masterful.'

Tindale threw his legs wide and jabbed his spurs into the horse's flanks. With a bound, the mare pranced forward, sprang up on its back legs and pitched Tindale to the ground.

Tindale drew the gun as he scrambled up, but Billy threw a running kick and the pistol went cartwheeling into the brush. While Billy was still on one foot, Tindale shouldered him, sent Billy rolling down the slope towards the quicksand hole. He grabbed roots and dirt and as his feet kicked up the slime, kicked the plank into the quicksand.

Billy craned up at Tindale who stood two yards back with fists clenched. He scrabbled at the roots, kicked quicksand, half hauled and half squirmed his way out of danger and up on his feet.

Billy crouched and Tindale's shoulders dipped while his fists came up and he waited for Billy's rush. He pivoted on one foot, but Billy changed tack and followed, snared a handful of shirt. Tindale's fists hit him fast as a drummer's ratatat. His scrambled brain didn't know which way was up and he crab-walked sideways till his right leg folded, dropped him on one knee. He came up immediately, shaking his head, and as he spun round brought up a fist to meet Tindale with.

But Tindale stood where he'd left him, in an easy crouch, fists just bobbing gently at the ready.

Billy slowly straightened a little more, and both men crouched, six feet apart, eyeing each other, taking stock.

They both had about the same few inches over six feet. Billy was wider, undoubtedly stronger. He didn't think he'd ever tested his strength to the full, maybe he was afraid to, as if those great slabs of muscle in his back, once really started to strain in earnest, could break his own bones, tear his ligaments apart — sometimes, though, he felt he could straighten his back under a bull.

But Tindale was strong too. He had the supple strength of a big cat, the kind that surges to full power in an instant. His fists were like a couple of pistons, hitting straight and fast. Where Billy might knock your head off, he'd shake up your brain till your thoughts whirled like snowflakes in a glass ball paperweight. And he'd got guts and will. He believed in himself — he wasn't about to fold up because deep down he thought he'd got it coming.

Neither had the pure killer instinct that makes some men so dangerous. But the two-legged beast of prey is as swift to avoid as strike — it knows when to back off, and will if the risk's too great. These two had men's unwise courage, and neither would back down or ever give up.

They edged in closer, cautious but not afraid. The horse tossed its head and rolled its eyes, and the kid, eyes flinching, backed away, unable to stand within the aura of raw power that surrounded the two men.

Tindale swayed back, gathered himself, and slid forward, smooth enough to seem slow, but fast enough to rock Billy's head twice before he could react. And when Billy's sledgehammer whooshed through the air, Tindale had already eased back out of reach.

Tindale stalked around him, his hands only half closed and weaving the air, while Billy shifted on his feet, trying to keep him in sight — and then, without breaking stride, Tindale loomed closer and Billy was looking at a world gone dark at the edges and flecked with floating sparks.

He tried to close, rather than stand there and let Tindale pick him off, but it was like trying to catch a floating feather where the wind from your hand just blows it out of reach. Then as he was sliding away, like a leopard that changes direction with a convulsive jolt and dart, Tindale would be on him and as those fists pounded ratatat Billy would see his blood fly like spray when a wet hound shakes its muzzle.

Tindale circled, fists bobbing easily at the ready. There was no need to take chances. He just had to wait and pick the shot that would finish it.

Billy staggered round, like a wounded bull wearied by the jabs that madden it and sap its strength for the kill. His head felt light and huge. He could only see out of one eye, the right was full of blood. He coughed and hawked his right canine out of his throat, spat it and a gout of blood on the ground. Then he dragged his fist up from his knee and lumbered in.

Each swing of a big fist that cleaved empty air sapped him a little more. Tindale's chest was rising and falling, but he was breathing through his nose.

Billy's hot breath scorched his throat, blew bloody foam from the corners of his mouth. If his left eye closed any further, he'd have to fight by smell alone. He squinted at Tindale standing just always out of reach, handsome, debonair, his face unmarked and breathing no harder than if he'd just got done with a brisk waltz, and he saw himself: big toothless chops gaping as he tried to eat enough air to satisfy his lungs, half blind and dripping blood, and shuffling like some tired old bear made to dance — and the humiliation dragged his heart down even more than the pain of his wounds or the weariness of his body.

Billy heaved up his fists and roared and lumbered towards Tindale. Tindale's fist pistoned into his face, then as he slipped back out of reach, a foot slid on slick weeds and dropped him on one knee. Billy's roundhouse swing connected as he bounced back up, lifted him off his feet, hurled him with a dull clap into the quicksand.

19

Billy's follow through swung him right round. Brush and sky swam past his one good eye and the quicksand slapped his back so the air whooshed from his lungs, then it began to swallow him whole.

'Billy, get the rope,' Mike called. 'Get the rope, Little Billy.'

The boy picked up the lasso and ran to the bank's edge. He pulled out the noose and hesitated. He looked at Tindale, then looked at Billy.

'One of us is done for,' Tindale said. His arms were stretched out over the quicksand that reached to his chest. The fingertips of his right hand were inches from the fingers of Billy's left.

The boy ran to his left, closer to Billy, — was about to throw him the noose when, sudden and electric as lightning stabbing the sky, came a yell.

'Wait.'

The boy froze, turned his face up to the girl.

'He's your father, Billy.'

The boy's head turned, and he gazed at Tindale with eyes that were as unfocused as a blind man's.

'He's your father,' the girl cried. 'Help him.'

The boy's head turned from one to the other: to Billy, one eye blind, the other no more than a slit, face covered in blood like red lacework; to Tindale — in whose grey eyes the essence of his being was concentrated in a moment of dreadful intensity.

'Mama — '

'Danny,' the girl wailed and her hands flew to her face.

The rope slapped down on the slime within reach of Billy's hand.

'Tie it to the horse, Billy,' Mike called. 'Tie the rope round the horse's neck.'

The kid ran to the horse and tied the rope to it with a big double knot.

Billy pulled the noose over his head, worked his arms through. The boy tugged on the bridle, and the horse took the strain of the rope, dipped its head, and began to pull.

'Danny,' the girl screamed.

'Don't look, Milly,' Tindale said. The slime was up to his chin now.

'Oh, Danny.'

'Look away, girl,' Tindale said. 'Oh, dear God . . . '

Mike grabbed the girl and pulled her down, pushed her face into his chest and covered her ears as Tindale began to gag and retch.

20

Billy dragged himself to his feet, though muscle, nerve and bone begged for rest. He hoisted the boy onto the horse, then climbed up himself and searched until he found a dry way through the brush. Blind, with Mike's shouts to guide him, he made his way to where they waited on the other side of the pit.

Mike and Carter rode the horse, and they picked their way through the treacherous marsh, winding this way and that and covering distance at a snail's pace, until following the faint remains of a track led them to a cabin in a glade.

'We'll stop here,' Mike said. 'Rest for the night. You need rest.'

'I can go on,' Billy said tramping on, hunched and surly.

But Mike said, 'We'll stop.'

They wrestled with the door till it

swung open on its leather hinges, and crowded inside, leaving a confusion of footprints in the dust. Billy stripped the rotten blanket from the cot and threw it in the corner, then spread his bedroll over the stuffed sacks that served as a mattress. The girl obeyed Billy's touch on her arm, let herself be led to the cot, and sat down. She sat with face blank and eyes lowered, motionless except for a slight tense tremor of the eyelids.

'You lay down and rest,' Billy said. His voice was weak and apologetic and she didn't respond to it, but when he touched her shoulder she obeyed again, automatically as before, and lay back and turned her face to the wall.

'This could be the place where that crazy miner lived,' Carter said. 'What do you think?' Carter turned to Billy who sat beside him at the table, but Billy didn't even seem to hear, just sat hunched at the table, mouth open showing his gums, staring at his hands as if he'd never seen anything like hands before but was trying hard to work out what they were.

'I said — '

'Keep quiet,' Mike said.

'You guys are a heap of fun.'

Carter stood up and wandered about the cabin. There wasn't much to see: just the cot and a box-stool beside it, the table and two benches, pegs wedged between the wall timbers to hang a coat and a hat.

'A message,' Carter said, leaning over the girl. 'I wonder if it's from the crazy miner. Lost on me, whoever it's from — never could read writin' no matter how hard I stare. Guess I'll get some sleep.'

Carter picked himself a spot in the corner and, true to his word, was soon asleep to judge by the sound of his breathing.

The boy's eyes began to droop. Billy was already gone, his head resting on his arms on the table. Mike stood up and tried his bad leg. It hurt, but it held him. He picked up the boy and carried him over and laid him down beside his mother on the cot.

As he leaned over them he looked at the words etched with a knifepoint into the wall timbers beside the cot. The fading light, falling slantwise on them from the half-open door just about showed them up.

'And whatsoever mine eyes desired,' they read, 'I kept not from them. I withheld not my heart from any joy; for my heart rejoiced in all my labour: and this was my portion of all my labour.

'Then I looked on all the works that my hands had wrought, and on the labour that I had laboured to do: and, behold, all was vanity and vexation of spirit, and there was no profit under the sun.'

Lying on the boards beside the cot was the rusted old clasp knife that had no doubt carved the words.

Mike limped back to the bench, and folding his arms on the table lay his head on them.

★　★　★

Somewhere out in the glade a jay whistled, and Mike opened his eyes. A dim strip of grey light showed under the door. From the corner came the sound of Carter clawing breath over his tonsils and letting it back out with a little moan and a whistle. He could make out the dark bulk of Billy's head and shoulders on the table, and hear his deep, regular breathing, interrupted by a faint muffled honk from his blood-choked nose.

The tendons of his neck felt like rusted cables that had seized solid long ago, and when he tried to raise his head, the pain made him think again. He sat up, a cautious stage at a time. When he finally managed to get on his feet, he hobbled over to the door and eased it open on its leather hinges.

The glade was still and pale in the grey dawn, silent except for the jay letting the world know it was the big-shot round these parts. Mike wondered where Billy had tied the horse. He walked round the back of the cabin, but there was no sign of it, and when he got to the door again he saw what he'd noticed before without taking in: the track of trampled grass leading out of the glade.

He went back inside and saw that the kid lay alone on the cot. The saddlebags still lay in the corner. He checked them: the sacks of gold were still there.

'Where's she gone?'

Mike turned to see Billy staring at the cot.

'I don't know, but your horse is gone too.'

Billy rushed outside, making the cabin shake as his shoulder jolted the doorframe on the way.

'What's up?' Carter said.

'Never mind,' Mike said and followed Billy outside.

Billy stood in a half crouch, hands out from his sides, fingers hooked and ready, like a man about to tackle an invisible opponent.

Mike pointed to the tracks through the grass.

'There's where we came, and there's where she left.'

'Yeah . . . ' Carter stood scratching himself in the doorway ' . . . probably miles away by now.'

They heard the boy's sleepy voice calling his mama. Billy turned with a face like somebody had put a knife in his guts.

The boy squeezed out by Carter, and rubbing the sleep from his eyes, he squinted past his knuckles and said, 'Where's mama?'

'Your mama's taken off,' Carter said. 'There's the tracks as plain as day.' The boy looked from Carter to Billy, then his face beginning to twist up, he followed Carter's pointing finger.

'Mama,' the boy screamed and began to run.

Billy followed lumbering after the boy and reaching out grabbed his skinny shoulders.

'Leave me alone,' the boy cried. 'I want my mama.'

'Little Billy — '

'I ain't Little Billy,' the boy yelled. 'It's your fault she's gone. Put your hands off of me.'

Those arms of Billy's that could break a bear's back seemed to lose their strength. The boy squirmed free, and Billy stood there with his big hands hanging, as the boy ran down the track. When the vegetation swallowed him from sight, they could still hear him sobbing and pleading for his mother to come back.

I'm sick of this job, Mike thought.

He'd be glad to get to headquarters, make a report of these incidents, and have done with it.

THE END

Matt Matthews had carved his ranch out of the wild Wyoming frontier. But he had his troubles. The big blow of '86 was catastrophic, with dead beeves littering the plains, and the oncoming winter presaged worse. On top of this, a gang of desperadoes had moved into the Snake River valley, killing, raping and rustling. All Matt can do is to take on the killers single-handed. But will he escape the hail of lead?

THE WIND WAGON

Troy Howard

Sheriff Al Corning was as tough as they came and with his four seasoned deputies he kept the peace in Laramie — at least until the squatters came. To fend off starvation, the settlers took some cattle off the cowmen, including Jonas Lefler. A hard, unforgiving man, Lefler retaliated with lynchings. Things got worse when one of the squatters revealed he was a former Texas lawman — and no mean shooter. Could Sheriff Corning prevent further bloodshed?